Secret
Admirer

—⟨∽⟩—

Ruth Ann Nordin

This is a work of fiction. The events and characters described herein are imaginary and are not intended to refer to specific places or living persons. The opinions expressed in this manuscript are solely the opinions of the author and also represent the opinions or thoughts of the publisher.

Secret Admirer

All Rights Reserved.

Copyright 2023 Ruth Ann Nordin

V1.0

Design Credit: Book Wizz

This book may not be reproduced, transmitted, or stored in whole or in part by any means including graphic, electronic, or mechanical without expressed written consent of the publisher/author except in the case of brief quotations embodied in critical articles and reviews.

Chapter One

January 1830

Lady Rachel waved her fan to help cool herself off. The ballroom was full, and more than half the people were dancing. Her gaze went to the available bachelors, most of whom she'd already danced with since starting her Season. Unfortunately, not a single one interested her.

She turned to her two friends. "How are we supposed to pick a gentleman if not a single one interests us?"

"I think we're supposed to pick the one who has the most money," Miss Lydia Hamilton said. "Though," her gaze went to Lady Carol, "you might have already secured the wealthiest bachelor in London."

Carol shook her head. "I didn't secure him. My father did. And he did that when I was a child."

"Yes, but you must be pleased with the match," Lydia insisted. "He's gorgeous."

Rachel followed Lydia's gaze and saw Carol's betrothed who was scowling as someone talked to him. "I don't think the Duke of Augustine is happy tonight."

Carol rolled her eyes. "He's never happy. He looks at me like that all the time. I'm just glad I'm not the only one he scowls at. It assures me that there's nothing wrong with me."

"Of course, there's nothing wrong with you," Rachel said. "You're a lovely person. If you weren't, Lydia and I wouldn't be your friend."

Lydia gave another look at the Duke of Augustine. "Are you sure he's not scowling because he has something sharp stuck in his boot? Maybe it's lodged in there so tightly he can't get it out."

Carol shook her head. "You're much too nice. There's nothing stuck in his boot. He's just an unpleasant person. I don't know who enjoys being around him."

Lydia sighed. "What a shame. No one that good looking should be unpleasant to be around." She scanned the ballroom. "What about him, Rachel? He's not bad looking, and he's well dressed."

Rachel followed her friend's gaze and saw a blond-haired gentleman who was standing off to the side of the room. At first, she thought he was moving to the lively upbeat music, but then it occurred to her that he was fidgeting. Her eyebrows furrowed. Whatever was wrong with him?

"Does he seem unusual to you?" she asked her friends.

Lydia and Carol studied him. He seemed to realize someone was staring at him, for he looked in their direction. He jerked in panic. Rachel and her friends hurried to avert their gazes so as not to cause him more unease. She waited for a couple of seconds and chanced another look in his direction. He was gone. She searched for him and saw that he had moved to the doors of the veranda. When their eyes met, he gasped and hurried to open the door and slipped outside.

Lydia laughed. "You might have a harder time finding a husband than we expected if the gentlemen you look at bolt for the door."

Rachel stared in surprise at the veranda before directing her gaze to her friend. "I don't understand it. Won't he get cold out there?"

Lydia shrugged. "I have no idea what he was thinking when he ran off like that."

Rachel's brother, the Duke of Creighton, approached. "Did you notice anyone interesting?"

Ignoring the way Lydia chuckled, Rachel gestured to the veranda. "There was a gentleman I seemed to have made an impression on. He headed out of the ballroom when he realized I was looking in his direction."

Horatio's attention went to the gentleman who was standing outside. Just as she thought, he was getting cold out there. He was starting to shiver.

"You need to talk him into coming back inside," she said. "He seems uncomfortable out there."

"I'm sure he is, given how chilly it is," her brother replied. "But I'm not surprised you managed to chase him out of the room with a simple look. That's Lord Quinton." He patted her shoulder. "Just know that you're not the reason he ran. He's a bit odd, but he's a good gentleman."

"How do you know him?" Lydia asked.

"He's a member of White's. I see him there all the time," he replied.

Lydia glanced back at the veranda. "Is he wealthy?"

"Very," Horatio said. "But he's also skittish." His attention went back to Rachel. "I want to take you around the room and introduce you to a few people. Maybe we can find someone worth marrying you."

Rachel offered her friends an apologetic smile before she headed off with her brother. She hated leaving them, but she was here to find a husband. She'd have to wait until she was betrothed before she could fully enjoy herself at these balls.

"We have enough money," Horatio whispered, "so we don't have to be concerned with the gentleman's financial status. You have the benefit of choosing someone whose company you enjoy. Earlier today, you said you'd like someone with a sense of humor?"

"Yes, I love to laugh."

"What lady doesn't?"

She was sure all ladies wanted a gentleman who could make them laugh, but some, like Lydia, had to marry for money. "Are you sure you won't marry Lydia?"

He groaned. "Not this again."

"I'm sorry, Horatio, but I don't understand what you mean when you say she's like a sister. I'm your sister. She and I aren't that much alike, nor do we look alike."

"It's hard to explain. Perhaps if we didn't all grow up together, it would be different, but there's simply no way I can marry her."

Rachel sighed but didn't let him see how much his answer disappointed her. She had hoped that when she made the suggestion at the beginning of the Season, he would start to look at Lydia in a different way, but such wasn't the case. He was just as determined not to marry her as he'd been when she first mentioned it.

Horatio brought her to a group of people who were talking. Considering there were two couples who appeared to be in their thirties and one gentleman who was probably twenty, she guessed that her brother was hoping to match her up with the younger gentleman.

"I hope I'm not interrupting anything important, but I wanted to introduce my sister," her brother spoke up as soon they stopped talking to look their way.

"You're not interrupting anything, Your Grace," the older gentleman with blond hair said. "We were just discussing who might be a suitable lady to introduce my brother to."

"Then my timing is perfect." Horatio turned to her. "That is Lord Durrant and his wife. The other couple are Lord and Lady Worsley." To them, he added, "This is my sister, Lady Rachel. She's in her first Season."

The group offered her a greeting, which she reciprocated.

"My brother is Mr. Reuben St. George," Lord Durrant told Rachel. "He's still getting used to London. I'm here to make sure he doesn't get lost."

Mr. St. George rolled his eyes but chuckled. "I'm not a child anymore." His gaze went to Rachel and Horatio. "You get lost one time as a child while exploring the estate, and your older brother never lets you forget it."

The group laughed.

"You should be glad your brother cares so much about you," Lady Durrant said. "Not all brothers are as close as you two are."

"I am glad," he assured her. "I just wouldn't mind a little more freedom from time to time."

When the group stopped laughing, Horatio asked Lord Durrant, "Will you put in a suggestion at White's for him to become a member?"

"I might," Lord Durrant replied. "I want him to get used to being in London first. It's a lot different here than it is in the country. London is a big place. There are a lot of people."

"There's really not much to it," Lord Worsley spoke up. "As soon as you figure out where the main points of interest are, you've discovered all you really need to know. It's nice being in London. There's plenty to do for entertainment besides walking and reading all the time."

"There's more than that to do in the country, but I agree it's nice to have so much at your disposal in London," Lady Worsley chimed in.

"One thing you can do is dance with my sister, if you're inclined," Horatio inserted with a hopeful smile.

Rachel was wondering when her brother would get to his reason for bringing her over here. Sometimes she didn't know who was more excited about her Season. While she anticipated finding that special someone she was going to spend the rest of her life with, he was the one coming up with ideas on who might make her a good match. She appreciated his efforts, but there were times when it was a little embarrassing. She would have preferred it if Mr. St. George had asked her to dance. Out of politeness, he would dance with her. She didn't know if he agreed to the dance because he wanted to or if it was because her brother had suggested it.

Aware her brother watched her with that spark of hope in his eyes, she accepted Mr. St. George's arm and let him escort her to the dancing area. Her gaze went to her friends, and she saw the curious expressions on their faces. She offered a shrug. She didn't know what to think of

Mr. St. George yet. She'd just met him. Only time would tell if anything would come from meeting him.

Chapter Two

"Nothing came from meeting Mr. St. George," Rachel told her friends the next day as they sat in her drawing room. "In fact, nothing came from meeting any of the gentlemen last night. The whole ball would have been a waste of my time had you two not been there."

Lydia and Carol didn't hide their disappointment. "What was wrong with them?" Lydia asked.

"Nothing was wrong with any of them," Rachel replied as the butler set the tray of tea and crumpets down on the table near them. "They were all nice. I think I'm the one to blame for not being able to attract a suitor. Maybe I'm boring, or maybe I'm not pretty."

"Neither one is true," Carol argued. "You are a lot of fun to be around, and you are very pretty. You'd make a wonderful wife."

"If that's true, then why hasn't someone asked to be my suitor yet?" Rachel asked.

Carol shrugged as the butler poured tea into the cups. "Maybe they lack good sense."

Despite her disappointment over last evening, her friend's comment brought a smile to Rachel's face. This was why she most enjoyed her time with her friends. No matter how she was feeling, they always found a way to make her feel better.

"I haven't secured a suitor, either," Lydia said. "You're not the only lady languishing like a bouquet of wilted flowers in the corner of a room."

"Yes, but you need to marry for money," Rachel replied. "You're looking for someone specific."

"Not really. He just needs to be rich, handsome, and fun to be around." Lydia accepted the cup from the butler. "That's all."

Carol took the cup the butler held out to her. "That's a lot to ask of any gentleman. Why not compromise? Maybe he can be rich, not-so-handsome, and a bit dull?"

Lydia grimaced. "If I must save my family from financial ruin, I'd like to at least enjoy being married. You two are fortunate. You didn't have a father who squandered the family money."

Rachel accepted the cup from the butler. "Aren't your brothers trying to rectify that?"

"Yes, they are," Lydia said. "They managed to pay off the family's debts. But now we have very little left for the estate."

"At least you have an estate," Rachel replied as the butler left the room. "Land is worth something."

"Land can't buy the little luxuries we've taken for granted." Lydia took a sip of her tea. "I'm just as spoiled as they are. I like to spend money on things like gowns, delicacies, and entertainment."

"Your brothers buy gowns?" Carol teased.

Lydia shook her head at her friend. "Very funny, Carol."

Rachel giggled. "You have to admit the idea of them in gowns does bring up certain images in the mind."

"Certain *hideous* images, you mean," Carol added with a chuckle.

Lydia gagged. "I'm trying to enjoy our refreshments." She picked up a crumpet. "I accidently saw one of them improperly attired one evening and thought I was going to have to gouge my eyes out."

Rachel gasped. "When did this happen?"

"A year ago when he got drunk and thought it'd be funny to go through the entire townhouse with only his drawers on. He must have thought he was fighting a dragon because he kept screaming that he was going to save some damsel in distress while wielding a cane like a sword." Lydia shivered. "It was horrible. To this day, the maid and butler chuckle whenever he enters the room."

"Why didn't you tell us about this before?" Rachel asked. She glanced at Carol to make sure Lydia hadn't told Carol about this, and she was assured that this was the first Carol was hearing of the incident, too.

"Why would I want you two to know something like that?" Lydia asked.

"Because it's funny," Rachel replied.

"It isn't funny," Lydia said. "In fact, it was embarrassing. If our father hadn't arranged for the maid and butler to be paid by a lawyer for the rest of their lives, I doubt they would still be with us to this day." She shivered again. "I just want to forget it ever happened." She bit into her crumpet.

"Which brother was it?" Rachel asked.

"I'm not saying," Lydia replied.

"Does he still get drunk?" Carol asked.

Lydia shook her head. "Thankfully, he recalled the incident and hasn't had a drink since."

Carol's gaze went to Rachel. "It was Felix. Felix rarely drinks brandy anymore."

Lydia opened her mouth to protest but then groaned. "Ugh. I wish you hadn't figured it out. You're much too clever."

Rachel thought for sure it was Oscar since he wasn't as serious about things as Felix was. Imagine Felix getting so drunk he thought he was fighting a dragon. She was glad her brother didn't act like that.

She caught sight of someone coming into the room and directed her attention to the butler. He was holding a missive.

"This came for you, Lady Rachel," he said and held it out to her.

She accepted the missive, thanked him, and waited until he left before she opened it. The contents were brief, but they made her pulse race in excitement.

"Who is it from?" Lydia asked when she finished her crumpet.

Rachel's gaze went to the bottom of the missive, and she frowned. "I don't know."

Lydia wiped her fingers on the cloth napkin. "How can you not know? Didn't the person sign it?"

"Well, he did, but he didn't give his name." Rachel inspected the envelope but didn't see anything to identify the writer of the missive there, either. "He signed it, 'Your admirer.'"

Carol perked up in interest. "You received a love note from a secret admirer?"

Lydia's eyes lit up, and she gestured to the parchment in Rachel's hand. "What does it say?"

Rachel's cheeks warmed. "It's a bit personal."

"In that case, wait." Lydia jumped up and ran to shut the door. She sat back down and gave Rachel her full attention. "I don't want to miss anything. Go on."

Rachel chuckled. "I suppose I can share this with you. All right." She cleared her throat. "He wrote, 'I hope you don't mind that my confession comes on parchment rather than in person, but I had to express my feelings somehow. Lady Rachel Abbot, there is no lady lovelier than you. No one can match you in beauty or in kindness. At night, I dream of you and wish for a future where we might be together. There will never be anyone for me but you. I will always and forever be your devoted admirer.'"

"And…?" Lydia prompted.

"That's all he wrote." Rachel placed the parchment in her lap. She was going to have to keep it. She'd never received anything this wonderful before.

"Don't you want to know who wrote it?" Lydia asked. "If I got something like that, I'd want to know who wrote it."

SECRET ADMIRER

"Of course, I want to know who wrote it," Rachel began, "but there's no way I can find out. The sender didn't give me his name or title."

"Ooh, how romantic," Carol said. "I think it's nice that you don't know. It makes it more mysterious. He could be anyone who was at the ball last night."

"I don't like the mystery of it." Lydia's gaze went to Rachel. "I want to know who sent it."

Rachel laughed. "Read it for yourself. You won't find any clues there."

Lydia accepted the missive and looked it over for a good minute before she groaned in frustration. "He didn't leave any clues. You'd think the least he could do is leave his initials. Then we could ask around London to see if we can find out who he is."

"I think the point of the anonymous note is to avoid finding out who sent it," Carol pointed out.

"Carol's right," Rachel said. "He didn't sign it because he doesn't want me to know his identity. It's sweet that he wrote to me." She took the missive and smiled. "This is going in my box of treasures."

Lydia rolled her eyes. "What good is having an admirer if he isn't going to be your suitor?"

When Lydia put it like that, Rachel supposed she had a point. Maybe it would be nice to know who the sender of this missive was. "I don't even know how to start finding out who this gentleman is."

"You could start with the butler," Lydia suggested.

Rachel's eyebrows furrowed. "The butler?"

"He was the one who gave you the missive," Lydia said. "Surely, he got it from someone. That might be the person we should track down. He might be a servant of the gentleman who's besotted with you."

Rachel read the missive again. It would be nice to know who thought so well of her. Who knew how many times she might have walked right by him and not know it? Maybe she had even danced with him. If she danced with him, she would have talked to him.

"All right," Rachel decided. "I'll ask the butler about it. Then we'll see if we can find out who sent it."

MR. EDWIN MORGAN SELECTED two bottles of wine that his master, Duke of Creighton, had requested for that evening's meal. He tucked the bottles under his arm, retrieved the candle, and walked up the cellar steps. Once at the top, he closed the door and locked it. Then he placed his keys in his pocket and headed down the hall.

Mrs. Abigail Brown, the head housekeeper, happened to be coming from the opposite direction.

"Did Mark ever catch that rat?" he asked her.

She offered him a smile. "Yes, thankfully, it went right into the trap he set out."

His eyebrows rose in surprise. "Your son ought to be congratulated on a job well done."

"I already gave him a piece of candy."

"You did? What kind?"

"A lemon drop."

"What a lucky lad."

"It's his favorite," she said. "It was the least I could do from saving us all from embarrassment. The last thing we need is for the master to find out a rodent found its way into this place."

"That would be bad news, especially on a day when he's having a dinner party."

"Yes. Now we can focus on getting everything ready."

He nodded in agreement then continued on his way to his office. He set the wine bottles and candle down then sat at the small desk. He opened the ledger so he could record the fact that he'd taken the wine from the cellar. He made a note to order more wine then placed the lid back on the inkwell.

When he noticed that the top drawer of the desk was slightly open, he hurried to close it. In his haste to write the missive to Lady Rachel, he had forgotten to close it all the way. Thankfully, no one ever came into this room, or they might have noticed the slip. He took a deep breath and released it. In all of his twenty-seven years of life, he'd never done anything so foolish.

His intention was only to give Lady Rachel encouragement. She'd seemed so despondent about not receiving any suitors. She was a lovely lady. She should know someone was attracted to her. For the life of him, he couldn't understand why she didn't have any gentlemen coming by to visit her.

It hadn't been until recently that he'd developed an affection for her. He had started out as a footman in this household when he was sixteen. She'd been seven. He remembered that because it happened to be her birthday, and her father had arranged for a party to celebrate it.

Edwin moved his way up to being the butler by the time he was twenty-five. Then her father died, and her brother stepped into his role as the duke. The transition worked well, though the year had been a somber one. Once the mourning period was over, her brother made arrangements to get her ready for her first Season.

It was the day Lady Rachel made her appearance at court that Edwin realized she wasn't a child anymore. She had grown into a lady. He'd never forget how beautiful she looked in the drawing room as she waited for her brother to escort her out of the townhouse. Try as he might, Edwin couldn't go back to thinking of her the same way he had before. And that had changed everything.

He couldn't do anything about his attraction to her, of course. She was a noble lady, and he was a servant. His job was to stay out of the way, only to approach her when it was necessary.

He could only hope that his missive had assured her that she was desirable. Sometimes all a person needed was to know someone believed in them in order accomplish something great. Her brother was a good master, but Edwin would always have a special amount of respect for her father since it was her father who saw to it that he was groomed into the job of being a butler. Her father saw potential in him that no one else ever had. Maybe his secret admiration of Lady Rachel could lead her to a gentleman deserving of her.

Feeling better, he released his breath. Lady Rachel didn't know the missive was from him. He'd been careful to leave no clues. As far as she was concerned, the missive could have come from anyone. He hadn't, unwittingly, upset things with his master. The last thing he'd ever do was act inappropriately toward his master's sister.

He straightened up in the chair and checked through the list of wines in stock. Everything was in order. All he had to do was replace the ones he would be using that evening. Then he would go to his pantry and retrieve the dishes to be used for the evening. He stood up, selected the key he needed, and headed for the pantry.

Chapter Three

"I invited a couple of bachelors to this evening's dinner party," Horatio said as he escorted Rachel into the drawing room. "I've been assured that they're all respectable gentlemen." He stopped her at a chair and gestured for her to sit. "I thought it might help ease your nerves if one of your friends was here. Since Carol is already betrothed, I thought I'd invite Lydia." He winked at her. "Who knows? Maybe one of the gentlemen here tonight will be her future husband."

Despite feeling too anxious about the evening to drink anything, she accepted the tea from the butler and thanked him. She didn't know if one of the guests this evening might be her admirer. So far, she hadn't gathered the courage to mention the admirer to her brother.

She released her breath and forced herself to take a sip of the tea. It had a hint of sweetness in it. Honey, if she guessed right. She loved the combination of black tea and honey. She wondered if her brother had requested it or if the butler thought to have it prepared for her.

Her brother sat next to her and drank his tea before he said, "There will be three gentlemen here this evening. One is Lord Wright. He's a widower with a child. The second is Lord Quinton. He's the one you and Lydia saw escape onto the veranda at the ball the other night."

She nodded. Yes, she remembered him. Thinking back on how skittish he was, she was tempted to chuckle. She doubted he was her secret admirer. The script in the missive hadn't been jagged in any way. It had been smooth. So her admirer probably wasn't the skittish type.

"The last gentleman is Mr. St. George," her brother added.

Her eyebrows rose in interest. Maybe Mr. St. George was her admirer. Maybe she had gained his interest at the ball but hadn't realized it.

She took a deep breath to help steady her nerves. "I'm glad Lydia will be here. It won't only help me relax a bit, but she's been having trouble finding a suitor, too. Unlike me, she needs someone who has money. Will any of these gentlemen be able to help her family?"

"Yes, all of them have more than enough wealth."

Good. That was perfect. Even if nothing came of this evening for her, maybe her friend would benefit from it. She cleared her throat. "What other ladies will be in attendance this evening?"

"Lord Wright has a sister and a cousin who will be here this evening," Horatio replied. "His sister is in her second Season, and she lives with him. His cousin, however, recently arrived here from Canada. She's in her late twenties. Given her age, I'm not sure if she'll appeal to anyone in attendance this evening." He shrugged. "If you add me, there will be four gentlemen here. I want all of the gentlemen to have someone to escort to dinner, so I asked Lord Wright to bring his cousin here tonight."

"How well do you know Lord Wright? I don't recall hearing about him before."

"He's an acquaintance. I've only talked to him a couple of times. Lord Durrant—that is Mr. St. George's brother—recommended him. I confided to Lord Durrant about Lydia's situation, and he thinks Lord Wright will be a good match for her."

"So who will you escort to dinner? Lord Wright's sister or cousin?"

"Since I'm older than Lord Quinton, I'll escort the cousin. He will escort the sister. After dinner, the gentlemen will join me in the den while you and the ladies will come in here. That should take a half hour to an hour, depending on how good the conversation is. Then the gentlemen and I will join you and the ladies in here, and we'll play a game or two. If all goes well, we'll be up late. If not," he shrugged, "I'll find a reason to let them go home early. I'm really hoping for a good evening. It would be nice if this is the evening you acquire a suitor."

"I'll do my best."

He smiled. "I know you will. The gentleman who marries you will be very lucky."

Pleased by the compliment, she returned his smile. It was nice to know she had his support. It lessened her anxiety considerably.

The butler came into the room with a gentleman and two ladies. "Lord Wright, Miss Carnel, and Miss Jamison are here."

Rachel stood up with her brother and greeted the guests as they came farther into the room. Lord Wright seemed to be in his mid-thirties. He was attractive in his own right, she supposed, but there was a certain sorrow in his eyes that made her think he might not be ready for a second marriage. He must have really loved his wife. Miss Carnel turned out to be his sister, and she was considerably younger than him. If Rachel had to guess, she was close to her age. She had a sweet look about her that made Rachel think the two could be friends if they were allowed enough time to talk. Miss Jamison, the cousin, however, seemed a bit more reserved. Rachel wasn't sure she would ever feel comfortable with her.

"Have a seat," Horatio invited as the butler poured tea into their cups. "Lord Quinton and Mr. St. George will be here shortly." He waited until the butler was done before asking, "How are the three of you doing?"

As Lord Wright began answering him, Rachel felt the weight of someone's gaze on her. Curious, she glanced toward the doorway and saw that the butler was looking at her. He averted his gaze and slipped out of the room. Her eyebrows furrowed. That was strange. She didn't think he'd ever spent time watching her before. But then, he knew she had received that missive. Was it possible he knew the identity of her secret admirer? Did he know that her admirer was one of the guests this evening, and he was waiting to see if she would figure it out?

Her attention went back to Lord Wright. He was talking about something his two-year-old daughter had done earlier that day. He didn't glance her way once while talking. She didn't think he was her admirer. Not only did she not know him, but he wasn't showing the slightest bit of interest in her. Her admirer must be one of the other two gentlemen who were due to arrive.

She took a deep breath and released it. Thankfully, her brother could keep a conversation going. She would be lost if he wasn't there. While she didn't consider herself to be shy, knowing her secret admirer might be here this evening did make her more cautious about what she should say and do. The last thing she wanted to do was lose the admiration of someone who held her in such high esteem.

"Lord Wright said you came here from Canada," her brother told Miss Jamison. "I hope you're enjoying your time in London."

"I am," Miss Jamison replied. "My cousins have been very kind in arranging for me to come here."

Rachel wanted to ask what prompted her to come to London but wondered if that was too personal, so she decided to keep her mouth shut.

"How did you handle the trip across the ocean?" her brother asked. "I heard some people get sick at sea."

"I managed all right, but a few people did take ill," she replied. "I was fortunate."

"Some people don't just get sick at sea," Miss Carnel spoke up. "Some get sick in a carriage. I don't like going to the country estate because all the swaying back and forth in the carriage makes me nauseous."

"Yes, we learned that the hard way when she was a child," Lord Wright added.

"How awful," Rachel said. "If that happened to me, I wouldn't leave London. It takes us four days to reach our country estate."

SECRET ADMIRER

"For us, it's three days." Miss Carnel rolled her eyes. "Three very loooong days." Then Miss Carnel put her hand over her stomach and pretended to gag.

Rachel's lips curled up in amusement. Even if Miss Carnel didn't fare well during those trips, she had a sense of humor about it. Rachel liked her. Lydia and Carol might like her, too.

The butler brought a gentleman into the room, and it took Rachel a moment to recognize him. He was the same one who had run out to the veranda when he realized she and Lydia were looking at him.

"Lord Quinton has arrived," the butler told the group. "I expect Mr. St. George to be here soon. I believe I saw his carriage pulling up to the townhouse on my way here."

Rachel thought he glanced her way, but he left the room within the next moment, so it was hard to tell. It was truly a strange thing. How often had the butler been in the same room with her, but she hadn't really noticed him?

Horatio stood up and gestured for Lord Quinton to join them. "I'm glad you're here."

As her brother proceeded to introduce them, Rachel noticed the way Lord Quinton kept patting the pocket of his waistcoat. Given the fact that his tailcoat covered most of his waistcoat, she couldn't make out what was in the waistcoat pocket. Whatever it was, he seemed worried he might lose it. Her brother was right about him; he did seem a bit odd. But odd was something one could overlook if the gentleman was nice.

Just as Lord Quinton sat down, the butler brought Mr. St. George into the room. This time, Rachel was assured the butler did glance in her direction as he introduced them to Mr. St. George. Her eyes widened in interest. Perhaps the butler was giving her a hint. Maybe Mr. St. George was her secret admirer.

Her heartbeat picked up as Mr. St. George joined the group.

"I hope I'm not late," Mr. St. George said.

"No, you're right on time," her brother replied. He quickly made the introductions then gestured for Mr. St. George to sit in the chair closest to Rachel. "We're waiting for one more guest. In the meantime, you've already met my sister."

Mr. St. George offered her a nod and a smile. "Yes, I had the pleasure of dancing with her at the last ball."

Well, that settled it. He had to be her secret admirer. Despite what she'd thought, he hadn't been bored while they danced. He'd just been shy. Feeling a bit shy herself, she offered him a smile in return.

Lord Quinton scanned the ladies, and he, once again, patted whatever was in his pocket. "Which lady will I be escorting to dinner?"

"Miss Carnel," her brother answered. "I will be escorting Miss Jamison. Lord Wright will escort Miss Hamilton, and Mr. St. George will escort my sister."

Lord Quinton took a careful look at Miss Carnel, and her eyebrows rose in surprise. Rachel couldn't blame her. What was he looking for?

"I can't help but notice the amulet you're wearing." Lord Quinton pointed to the small blue and green object that was pinned to her gown. "Is that supposed to be the eye of a peacock feather?"

Miss Carnel glanced down at the object. "No. And it's not an amulet. It's a cameo."

He took another good look at it then relaxed. "All right. I'll be happy to escort you to dinner."

Rachel glanced back at Miss Carnel. The two made eye contact, and Miss Carnel gave Rachel a questioning look. All Rachel could do was shrug. She didn't have the slightest idea as to why Lord Quinton was worried about the cameo.

The butler returned to the room, and this time he brought Lydia with him. Rachel smiled, glad her friend had finally made it.

"Miss Hamilton, Lord Wright will be your escort to dinner this evening," her brother said after he introduced her to the group.

SECRET ADMIRER

Rachel thought it was funny he should refer to Lydia so formally when they had grown up together, but considering the fact that they were surrounded by strangers, she understood why he'd done it. She just hoped she didn't slip and call her friend Lydia until after dinner. After dinner, things would be more relaxed.

Lydia settled into her chair.

"Can we change the ladies we escort to dinner?" Lord Quinton asked.

Shocked he should ask the question, Rachel's gaze went to her brother. She might be new to these dinner parties, but she was sure this kind of thing didn't happen a lot. Poor Miss Carnel. This had to be embarrassing for her. She offered Miss Carnel an apologetic smile.

Horatio moved his mouth for a moment but no sound came out. Finally, he cleared his throat. "It's just dinner, my lord."

"Yes, but dinner can set the tone for the rest of the evening." Lord Quinton, once again, patted his pocket. "It's nothing personal against Miss Carnel. She's a very attractive lady. It's just that she is wearing that cameo. Even though it's not the eye of a peacock, it's a bit unsettling. You see, the eye of a peacock is unlucky."

"Do you want me to take it off?" Miss Carnel asked.

"Oh, I would never tell a lady to remove her cameo," Lord Quinton replied. "That would be rude."

Rachel's eyes grew wide. That would be rude, but asking to escort another lady to dinner wouldn't be?

Horatio glanced between Lord Quinton and Miss Carnel. "Well, I don't wish to be a bad host."

Miss Carnel's cheeks grew pink, but she offered a polite smile. "It's all right with me if another gentleman escorts me to dinner. I don't mind."

Rachel winced on her behalf. She had to have minded. If Rachel's escort asked to be with someone else, she would be so embarrassed that she'd want to leave the room.

21

"Thank you," Lord Quinton told her. "That's very gracious of you, Miss Carnel." Not hiding his relief, he turned to Lydia. "I'll escort you."

Lydia's eyebrows furrowed. "Why me?"

"Your hair is a pleasant blond color, and your last name isn't close to the word 'carnal'. Also, you're wearing a pink gown. Miss Jamison is wearing red, so I don't feel comfortable picking her. Lady Rachel's hair is so dark that it's like raven wings. Of all the ladies in attendance, you are the best choice." He spoke in such a matter-of-fact way that Rachel would have chuckled if she didn't feel so bad for Miss Carnel.

"But Miss Hamilton is supposed to be my dinner companion," Lord Wright spoke up. "I don't mean to be impolite, but I can't escort my sister to dinner."

"Why don't you escort another lady then?" Lord Quinton asked.

Lord Wright turned his bewildered expression to Horatio. Horatio, in turn, glanced at Rachel with a question in his eyes. Rachel knew she was the only lady who could be paired up with him. She wasn't his cousin, and she wasn't his sister. As much as she hated to do it, it was the only way to ensure the evening went smoothly.

She reluctantly turned her gaze to Mr. St. George. "In light of recent events, would you mind if Lord Wright escorted me to dinner this evening?"

Mr. St. George offered her an understanding smile.

"I don't mind."

What a relief. He wasn't upset with her.

With a glance at Miss Carnel, Mr. St. George added, "It'll be my pleasure to escort you to dinner. I happen to like the colors blue and green."

"It's not the combination of blue and green that I don't like," Lord Quinton said. "It's the way the colors were put together. Doesn't anyone else see the eye of a peacock in that piece of jewelry she's wearing?"

"The eye of a peacock would be on a feather, not a cameo," Lord Wright pointed out.

SECRET ADMIRER

"That thing was made by someone," Lord Quinton said. "That someone could very well have intended for that thing to be the eye of a peacock."

Lord Wright seemed as if he was ready to respond but let out a loud sigh and shook his head.

Rachel didn't blame him for being annoyed with Lord Quinton. He had ruined things for them both. Now her secret admirer wouldn't escort her to dinner, nor would Lord Wright be Lydia's escort.

Poor Lydia was going to be stuck with Lord Quinton. That particular gentleman was more than odd. He was downright difficult. Thank goodness he hadn't asked to escort her. She didn't think she could have said yes. Then the dinner party would have been ruined for sure.

She would have to invite Lydia to go shopping with her as a way to make things up to her. Then they could stop by that shop which had those special candies Lydia enjoyed. Lydia didn't often get any sweets from there because they got expensive, but Rachel could afford to splurge on a few for her friend's sake.

"The other day, I heard the most marvelous joke," Horatio spoke up.

Everyone's attention went to him.

"There was a certain lawyer who became sick," her brother continued. "The malady he had was such a frightful thing that he created his will. In this will, he gave his estate to fools and madmen. When asked why he would give all of his possessions to fools and madmen, he said, 'They are the reason I have the estate, so I might as well give it all back.'"

The group laughed, and the mood in the room lightened considerably.

Chapter Four

Edwin probably shouldn't be glad that Lord Quinton put up such a fuss about Miss Carnel's cameo, but he was. It had forced Lady Rachel to be paired up with Lord Wright. She had no interest in Lord Wright. In his years of watching Lady Rachel, he had learned to detect subtle cues about her, and he'd noted the flicker of disappointment that crossed her face when she suggested that Mr. St. George escort Miss Carnel to dinner instead of her.

Edwin should want her to be with Mr. St. George. She did have a spark of interest in the gentleman. He wasn't sure if Mr. St. George shared the interest. He didn't know Mr. St. George. The subtle changes on his face were harder to interpret when he agreed to escort Miss Carnel. But the gentleman had been pleasant despite the upset Lord Quinton caused. Based on that alone, Edwin had to admit Mr. St. George was a good gentleman. It would be fitting if Rachel married someone like that. It should be something that would make Edwin happy. She would be getting someone who deserved her. And yet, he wasn't happy with the idea of her marrying him. All it did was create a silent panic deep inside him.

Forcing his mind off of her, he walked around the dining table to make sure the dinnerware was in order. When he was assured it was, he checked to make sure every candle was lit. There. Everything was perfect for the evening.

He gave a nod to the footman then left the room. When he reached the drawing room, he heard people laughing. He waited until the room grew quiet before he announced that dinner was on the table. Then he followed them to the dining room. Once everyone was seated, he presented the first course.

"Everything looks wonderful," Miss Carnel told Edwin's master.

"Yes, I must say this might be a pleasant dinner party after all," Lord Wright agreed.

Edwin pretended not to notice the slight scowl Lord Wright gave Lord Quinton. Lord Quinton, on the other hand, didn't have to pretend. He wasn't the least bit aware that Lord Wright was upset with him.

"I had Cook make dishes that I knew everyone would like," Edwin's master said, probably in an attempt to appease the tension between Lord Wright and Lord Quinton. "I managed to get fish for the main course."

"Cook does a marvelous job with the fish," Lady Rachel added.

Like their father, it was just like His Grace and Lady Rachel to pay compliments to the servants. It was why Edwin enjoyed his employment as much as he did. He'd heard horror stories from servants who served under ungrateful families. All they could do was wait for an opening in a better household to come up then apply to work there. Edwin couldn't help but feel sorry for them. He truly lucked out when Lady Rachel's father hired him. Back then, he hadn't known any better. He'd just been glad he had a job other than cleaning chimneys.

He handed the covers to the servants. With the first course ready, he went to the sideboard to wait for his master to tell him to pour the wine.

"Fish is a fine choice," Mr. St. George said. "At my country estate, there's a lake, and I've managed to catch a few good ones that my family's cook prepared for my mother and me."

"You did?" Lady Rachel asked.

Edwin's gut tightened. Did that impress her?

SECRET ADMIRER

Mr. St. George nodded. "My brother caught some, too. The lake is my favorite spot on the property. Fishing with my brother made it even better."

She gave Mr. St. George a smile Edwin would love to see her give him. "I think it's wonderful you and your brother have such a close relationship."

"Your brother is quite a bit older than you, isn't he?" His Grace asked Mr. St. George as he gestured for Edwin to serve the wine.

Edwin stepped up to the table and did as his master wished.

"In some ways, he's like a father to me," Mr. St. George admitted. "I don't remember my father. He died when I was still young. My brother took over the family estate and went to London to provide for my mother and me. I can't tell you what a treat it was when he came back for visits."

Edwin resisted the urge to sigh. Mr. St. George, it seemed, was very much the ideal suitor. Kind. Dedicated to family. Attractive. Yes, Lady Rachel would be very happy with him.

"We have a stream by our country estate," Miss Carnel spoke up. "I remember seeing a frog or a snake while sitting by it, but I don't recall any fish."

"If there were fish, they would have been too small to eat," Lord Wright said.

Miss Carnel nodded in a thoughtful manner. "That's true. A fish needs to be a good size if we can eat it." She glanced at Mr. St. George. "How big were the fish at your lake?"

While Mr. St. George told her, Edwin returned to his place at the sideboard with the wine bottle. He set it down then picked up the other bottle.

Dinner parties were rarely interesting enough to listen to. Most of the time, his mind wandered. But this particular dinner party was different. Lord Quinton seemed unusually interested in everything he drank and ate. Edwin tried not to keep looking over at him since he ought to be focused on his master, but Lord Quinton was the strangest gentleman he'd ever seen.

At the moment, he was sniffing the chestnut soup as if he wasn't sure if it was safe to eat. Lord Quinton glanced up at the ceiling for a long moment before he dipped the spoon into the bowl and took a sip of the soup. He didn't seem to know what to think of it since he hesitated to have more of it. Edwin would have worried there was something wrong with the soup if the others weren't consuming their soups with great enthusiasm.

Edwin heard a noise from the entrance of the dining room. He turned his gaze to the doorway and saw Mrs. Brown watching Lord Quinton. She probably hadn't meant to stare. From time to time, she would peek in to see if it was time to bring in the dishes for the next course. Usually, it would be about time for Edwin to use the cook's bell to let the other servants know their master and his guests were ready for the old dishes to be removed and the new ones brought in.

Mrs. Brown happened to look in Edwin's direction, so he shrugged. He had no idea why Lord Quinton seemed reluctant to eat the soup. She gave a surprised shake of her head and returned to the kitchen.

"Forgive me, Lord Quinton," His Grace said after the others had finished their soup. "I didn't realize you didn't like chestnut soup. I hope the Mackerel with fennel and mint and apple tarts will be more to your liking."

"Oh, I like the soup," Lord Quinton replied. "I was just trying to decide if the soup is cool enough to eat. It's bad luck to burn one's tongue." Then he proceeded to eat it.

Lord Wright glanced at Edwin's master, and in a low voice, he said, "I suppose we should be relieved he's more accepting of soups than he is of ladies."

Lord Quinton was far away enough not to overhear Lord Wright. It wasn't often that His Grace hosted a tense dinner party, but Edwin could see this would be a difficult evening for those in attendance. It was times like this that he was glad to be on the outskirts of events. No one would pay him any mind, and therefore, he would not be the focus of their displeasure.

Once Lord Quinton finished the soup, Edwin rang the cook's bell. Mrs. Brown and the others came in to take away the old dishes and to bring in new ones. Edwin removed the trays and served the food. Then, once more, he waited for his master to tell him when it was time to fill up the glasses with wine.

His Grace and Mr. St. George ended up doing most of the talking. The discussion revolved mostly around the different sights in London. Mr. St. George, it seemed, had spent most of his life in the country, so he was eager to find out what social activities he hadn't yet participated in. Lady Rachel voiced her enthusiasm over the menagerie, circus, and theatre. Edwin tried not to shift uncomfortably every time she glanced at Mr. St. George as if she hoped he would invite her to attend those outings with him in the future.

Toward the end of the dinner, it occurred to Edwin that Miss Carnel had begun to develop an affection for Mr. St. George as well. Edwin had to suppress the hope that Mr. St. George would pick Miss Carnel instead of Lady Rachel. *Lady Rachel is a noble lady. You're a servant, Edwin. Be mindful of your place.*

Edwin was relieved when His Grace indicated that he could finally leave the dining room. He went to the drawing room and the library to make sure the fires were roaring nicely in the fireplaces. Then he lit more candles.

Once the people in attendance left the dining room, Mrs. Brown and Mr. Hearty, the footman, found Edwin in his pantry. Edwin noted the way they were chuckling and knew exactly what they were thinking.

"No, I don't think I've ever come across anyone as odd as Lord Quinton, either," Edwin said before they could ask.

The two burst out laughing, but it was Mr. Hearty who said, "You missed the best part of the dinner. Lord Quinton wanted to know the exact ingredients in the pudding. It turns out there is some spice he's certain will bring him nightmares."

"Lord Wright said that having him at the dinner party was already a nightmare," Mrs. Brown added in a lower voice. "It's a good thing the two didn't sit next to each other, or Lord Quinton would have heard him."

"I didn't hear Lord Wright say that," Mr. Hearty replied.

"You were busy collecting the plates," she said. "I was only in the dining room because I had to tell Lord Quinton everything Mr. Samuel put into the pudding. Our poor cook. He thought our master was upset with the whole meal. I had to assure him the meal was fine."

Edwin winced. The cook had spent most of the day on the dinner. He was already worried that his older age might prompt their master to hire someone else. "I should tell him that Lord Quinton is a difficult gentleman."

"Oh, we already did that," Mrs. Brown assured Edwin before he headed for the door. "We explained all of the strange things Lord Quinton has been doing all evening. We're just glad the dinner is over. I don't know how much longer I could resist laughing around Lord Quinton."

"I have to see him again when he leaves," Mr. Hearty said. "I hope I can resist laughing." His gaze went to Edwin. "My lot is better than yours this evening. You have to give them tea if they want it."

Yes, Edwin was sure he would. Most of the time, his master would end the dinner party with some tea. Edwin didn't worry about laughing around Lord Quinton. He was too busy wondering how Mr. St. George would react to Lady Rachel. He took a deep breath then released it. It was going to be a long evening.

Chapter Five

"I feel sorry for you," Miss Carnel told Lydia once the ladies were relaxing in the drawing room after the meal was over.

Lydia's eyebrows furrowed. "Why?"

Miss Carnel's eyebrows rose in surprise. "Why else? Lord Quinton is not only strange, but he's obnoxious, too. I feel bad that you ended up with him as your escort."

Lydia shrugged. "He's just a little superstitious."

"A *little* superstitious?" Miss Jamison chuckled. "He was timid through the entire meal. One would think the cook was trying to poison him."

Miss Carnel giggled. "I'm sure the servants got a good laugh from how long he took to eat the soup."

Rachel gave the ladies an apologetic smile. "My brother had no idea he was so difficult. He thought Lord Quinton would make a good match for you, Miss Carnel. Lord Wright asked him to find someone with a pristine reputation to be your escort this evening. My brother had no idea he was so uptight. If he was in this room, he'd tell you how sorry he is."

Miss Carnel waved her hand. "Oh, it's fine. And call me Amelia. Now that we're not in a formal setting, there's no need to worry about formalities." Her gaze went to Lydia. "To be honest, I was glad Lord Quinton asked to be with you after he made all of that fuss over dinner. It was difficult to bear with him as it was. My concern is for my brother. He was looking forward to making your acquaintance. He's eager to get married again. He thought you would be his chance. But with Lord Quinton taking a liking to you, that's not going to happen." She glanced at Rachel. "I don't suppose you find my brother appealing?"

Rachel winced. "I'm sorry, but there's someone else I prefer."

Amelia gave her a hopeful expression. "Are you sure? He could use a mother for his child, and while he doesn't come out and say it, he gets lonely sometimes. I think when he is around gentlemen who have love matches, he gets depressed. Those gentlemen are happy."

"I met his wife once," Miss Jamison spoke up. "She was polite, but she wasn't friendly. There was a coldness about her."

"She didn't like London," Amelia said. "She liked to stay at the country estate. My brother, on the other hand, spent most of his time in London. He has so many investments that he could only go visit her a couple of times during the course of the year."

"That's a shame," Lydia said. "Hopefully, he'll find someone better the next time he marries."

"Are you certain you don't have an interest in Lord Wright?" Rachel asked Lydia. "Just because Lord Quinton escorted you to dinner, it doesn't mean you can't entertain a courtship with Lord Wright. Lord Wright is financially established. I'm sure he would be fine helping your family."

"My brother has plenty of money," Amelia agreed. "His investments have paid off beautifully. Sometimes I think all he touches turns to gold."

Rachel shot her friend an excited smile. That sounded even more promising. Horatio had done a wonderful job in selecting Lord Wright for her.

Lydia bit her lower lip. "Well, yes, it does seem like a good match, but I kind of fancy Lord Quinton."

Miss Jamison gaped. "You can't be serious."

Lydia's face turned pink. "I know he worries about silly things, but he's got a sweet way about him."

Miss Jamison shook her head in disbelief. "If you say so." Turning her attention to the others, she added, "It's a good thing he doesn't know my name. My name is Belladonna."

"What's wrong with that?" Rachel asked. "The name is quite lovely."

"Belladonna is also a deadly nightshade plant," she replied. "Can you imagine if Lord Quinton knew that? He wouldn't have gone anywhere near me lest I, like the plant, poison him."

"Oh, you're not giving Lord Quinton any credit," Lydia said. "You're a person, not the plant itself. He'd understand that."

Belladonna raised her eyebrows. "Are you sure? He thought Amelia was wearing a peacock eye, he doesn't like Rachel's hair because it's almost black like a raven. Then he didn't want to pick me because of my red gown. I'm guessing the red color makes him think of blood?"

Amelia shrugged. "It's hard to know why he hates that color."

"He's probably just a strange person," Rachel said. "Maybe some lady will be willing to overlook that strangeness because he's in the wealthier section of London."

Lydia turned to Rachel in interest. "He is?"

Rachel nodded. "My brother thought he'd fit right in with us because he's wealthy."

"Your brother is such a practical person," Lydia commented. "He doesn't believe in romance, though, does he?"

Rachel had never thought of her brother as a romantic, so it was hard for her to respond. She didn't see her brother the same way other ladies did. Lydia, on the other hand, had the potential to marry him, so she had a different view of him. Maybe it was just as well that Horatio had no interest in Lydia. By the tone in Lydia's voice, Rachel realized Lydia wanted a romantic husband.

"Better sensible than strange," Belladonna said. "I don't know how any lady could spend her life with Lord Quinton. All the money in the world can't make up for someone who believes every little thing around him might bring him bad luck."

"I agree. I'm glad I ended up with Mr. St. George," Amelia chimed in. "He didn't mind what I was wearing. Also, he did tell some interesting stories about his time at the lake on his estate, didn't he?"

"I enjoyed listening to him talk about the different fish he caught over the years." Belladonna chuckled. "I can't believe he shared the story about the time he fell into the lake, though. That must have been so embarrassing when it happened."

Amelia grinned. "That story was funny. I never laughed so hard in my entire life. He has a marvelous sense of humor. I didn't realize a gentleman could be so witty."

As the two continued to discuss the humorous event he had shared during the meal, Rachel's stomach tightened with dread. Amelia had taken an interest in Mr. St. George. She had wondered about that when Amelia asked him all of those questions during the dinner. Was it possible Mr. St. George returned her interest? If he was Rachel's secret admirer, that was before he met Amelia. Meeting Amelia might have changed things.

Well, there was no putting it off any longer. Rachel was going to have to talk to the butler. She had to find out if Mr. St. George was her secret admirer before she went into a full-blown panic.

EDWIN HAD JUST DISCUSSED the financial account with the steward to make sure he had sufficient funds to purchase more wine when he was summoned to the drawing room. Edwin frowned. Breakfast had been over for a good hour. He was certain he'd made sure everything had been cleared out and put away. Neither his master nor Lady Rachel were in the habit of seeking his services this time of day. Usually, both were in their bedchambers by now.

SECRET ADMIRER

Pushing aside his unease, he placed the sum of money he would take to the market in his pocket and hurried to the drawing room. It turned out Lady Rachel was the one who was waiting for him. That was a relief. Only his master would mention something he had missed during the breakfast. The fact that it was Lady Rachel who had summoned him, however, meant he would have to talk to her. And that caused him anxiety for a completely different reason.

He cleared his throat before approaching her. "Did you require my assistance with something, Lady Rachel?"

"Yes, thank you for coming." She checked the doorway to make sure no one was there before gesturing for him to come further into the room. In a low voice, she added, "I need to ask you something."

He glanced over his shoulder. Yes, she had looked at the doorway, but he hadn't. It was empty. For the moment, they were alone. He turned his gaze back to her. He didn't realize being alone in a room with her would make him feel so strange. He'd never been alone with her before. Every other time, she had been with her brother or one of her friends.

He felt like he was going to be sick to his stomach and spin around in excitement at the same time. Steadying his nerves, he prompted, "What is it?"

"You gave me a missive the other day," she said in a soft voice. "That happened to be a note from someone who secretly admires me. Do you know who sent that missive?"

Edwin was certain his heart stopped beating. He waited for her to tell him that she knew he had written that missive. It took him a good half-minute before he realized she wasn't going to say the words he dreaded. He couldn't come out and tell her that the missive was from him. He was only a butler. She was a noble lady. He wasn't her equal. He was beneath her. So, what, exactly, should he say?

After searching for a good response, he finally said, "No, I'm afraid I don't. A lad delivered it. I'm sure your admirer doesn't want to reveal his identity."

She didn't hide her disappointment. "I was hoping you might know. I thought perhaps it was Mr. St. George. He was supposed to escort me to dinner last evening, but then he couldn't. And as the evening went on, it seemed like he was interested in one of the other ladies. That's why I wondered if it was him who sent the missive. If not, then Mr. St. George's attraction to this other lady makes sense."

Surprised she would share this confidence with him, he hesitated to reply. So that meant the events that transpired after dinner hadn't gone as she'd hoped with Mr. St. George. Despite the fact that it was wrong, Edwin was happy to find this out.

"You don't need to worry about that," Edwin finally said. "The gentleman who sent that missive would never pick another lady over you."

Her eyes grew wide with hope. "You really think so?"

He knew so. He'd seen other ladies, and none of them equaled Lady Rachel in beauty or in kindness. A gentleman would have to be daft to resist her. Edwin was certain to die a bachelor since no one else could come close to her. And that was all right. Unlike titled gentlemen, he had no need to have an heir. His only legacy was his performance as a butler.

"I've worked in this household for many years," he began, "and you are the kind of lady your father hoped you'd be. Your father was a fine gentleman. It was an honor and a privilege to work for him. His opinion mattered a lot. If he was here right now, he'd tell you that if a gentleman fell in love with you, he wouldn't be able to stop."

She smiled. "That's very kind of you to say."

"It's not a matter of kindness if it's the truth. I wouldn't pay any mind to what happened with Mr. St. George. There is someone out there who holds you in the highest esteem. My advice is to think on that instead."

"Yes, you're right. That is the prudent thing to do." Her eyebrows furrowed. "I don't even know how to find out who my secret admirer is, though."

She really wanted to know who wrote that missive? Edwin might have meant the words he wrote on that parchment, but he never thought she'd want to discover the sender's identity. A pursuit like this would only complicate things.

"Lady Rachel," he began, "it's not my place to tell you what to do, but if this gentleman wanted you to know who he was, he would have signed his name. Why not just enjoy the missive? Is it not enough to know that someone thinks you're the loveliest lady in London?"

"I do enjoy the missive. I enjoy it very much. I'm sure it took him a lot of courage to disclose his feelings to me." She paused for a long moment. "I don't mean to burden you with my problems, but it's been such a frustrating Season. My brother has his hopes set on my getting married within the next few months, and so far, I've had no suitors. This missive is the closest thing I've gotten to one. I think this gentleman is the only one in London who's even attracted to me."

"That can't be true." She had to be wrong about that. There was no way that Edwin was the only person who saw her in a romantic light. "It's not easy for gentlemen to approach ladies. There's a lot of pressure involved. He has to figure out a way to be charming and good looking enough to appeal to her, and he has to hope he has enough money or influential connections to appeal to her father or brother. A lady's task, on the other hand, is easy. All she has to do is wait to be approached."

"One would think that would be easy, but it's not. I've spent a lot of evenings at the balls waiting for someone to talk to me or hoping my brother will find a suitable dance partner for me. I've done my best to pretty myself up, I made sure I took all of my dancing lessons, and I know more about how to conduct myself in polite society than anyone should know. Mr. St. George was the most promising prospect I had, but it turns out he's interested in Miss Carnel."

Edwin didn't know the details on what a noble lady went through in her Season, so he couldn't think of a good response to her words. All he knew was what it was like to be man who was in love with a lady he could never have. And that information wasn't going to help her.

"My secret admirer might be my only chance of securing a marriage," she continued. "Wouldn't it be good if I got to talk to him?"

He debated whether to say something, but since she was looking up at him in a way that made his heart beat faster, he blurted out, "It's possible you have talked to him without realizing it."

"I hadn't thought of that. But if I have talked to him, why hasn't he asked if he can be my suitor, or at the very least, why hasn't he asked if can pay me a visit?"

How could he possibly answer that? But he had to. She expected an answer. "Perhaps he's afraid you'll tell him no."

"Do gentlemen worry about things like that?"

"Of course, they do. A gentleman's heart is a fragile thing. It might not seem like it since society has gentlemen acting far braver than they are, but the lady he loves has the power to send him to the very heights of heaven by saying yes or send him to the very depths of despair by saying no. Everything depends on her response."

Her eyes grew wide. "I had no idea. It's no wonder he chose to hide behind the missive. I can't imagine saying no to someone who holds me in such high esteem, but he doesn't realize that."

Had he been a nobleman or even a well-to-do member of the middle class, her words would have made him come out and confess he wrote the missive. But he was just a butler. She couldn't say yes to someone like him. Society would forbid it.

"You have to help me figure out who he is," she said. "This gentleman is even more wonderful than I thought before I talked to you."

Good heavens. Did she really think that? "I don't know what I can do to help."

SECRET ADMIRER

"You're a butler. You can be in places I can't. You probably notice things I don't." She paused for a moment then smiled. "I'll talk my brother into hosting a ball! You can watch the gentlemen who attend. Surely, one of those gentlemen will give an indication of his longing to be with me. I bet you'd notice something I'd miss."

He shifted from one foot to another. "Maybe you should have your brother's help on this."

"My brother is a wonderful person, but he's not very good at picking up on subtle things."

"And you think I am?"

"I know it. You bring me tea before I tell you I want it, and you tend to the guests' needs before I have to request it. I notice you're also good about making sure the candles are lit when it's dark, and neither my father nor my brother have made a single complaint about the wine."

"It's my job to make sure everyone in this household is comfortable."

"Precisely. You've spent all of these years watching people and anticipating what they need. You catch things people like me and my brother miss."

He shook his head, ready to tell her he just couldn't do what she wanted when she put her hand on his arm.

"Please?" she asked in such a sweet tone that he lost his resolve.

He let out a sigh. "All right."

She squeezed his arm affectionately. "Thank you, Edwin! I realize my admirer is afraid of telling me who he is, but once I assure him I'm just as interested in him as he is in me, things will work out like they're supposed to."

She didn't know how she could make such a promise when she didn't know the person's identity, but by the look on her face, she was sincere. Edwin had an impossible time faulting her for believing she could ever be with her admirer. Just how was he going to get himself out of this mess?

Chapter Six

Rachel scanned the ballroom as the guests enjoyed the evening. As she'd hoped, her brother had agreed to host the event.

"I don't know why I didn't do this sooner," her brother confided as they took a moment to discuss how things were going. "Gentlemen are often drawn by wealth. Now that the bachelors see how much we can spend in one evening, I'm sure you'll have a suitor in no time."

Rachel didn't need to have a *suitor*, as her brother termed it. She needed to have her admirer. She couldn't even begin to guess which of the gentlemen in this room was the one. Certainly, he was here this evening. He cared for her too much to avoid coming here.

"I'm glad you thought of this," Horatio continued.

It was on the tip of her tongue to say that Edwin had inspired the idea, but she wondered if Edwin would want her to do that. She didn't know much about Edwin. He'd been working for the household for as long as she could remember. He hadn't always been the butler, but he had been among the staff. For the most part, he was in the background. She knew he was there to serve tea when her friends visited, and he assisted the other servants with the meals. But other than that, she had trouble knowing exactly what he did. That wasn't surprising, she supposed, since Edwin served directly under her brother.

Her gaze went to Edwin. He was opening a bottle of wine at the table where guests could get something to drink. Yes, he was the perfect person to watch what others were doing. He fit right in. Unlike her brother, he could blend into the background. She hadn't mentioned the admirer to her brother. At the moment, there was no reason to. Also, it might be a bad idea. Knowing how eager her brother was to secure her future, he might start going around the room and asking every bachelor if he was the one who sent her that missive.

"Between you and me, I'm relieved Lord Quinton decided not to come here tonight," her brother said, breaking her out of her thoughts.

Her gaze left Edwin and went to her brother. "He is an odd one, isn't he?"

"I was afraid if he came, there might be an argument between him and Lord Wright," her brother replied. "I was worried Lord Wright wouldn't even attend this ball, but, thankfully, he's here. I feel terrible about how poorly things went at dinner last week. I like Lord Wright. He's a good gentleman." He paused. "I don't suppose you have an interest in him, do you?"

Considering he wasn't her admirer, she shook her head. "No, I have no interest in him. I had entertained thoughts about Mr. St. George, but his affections aren't for me." She gestured to the spot where he was dancing with Amelia. "As awkward as things were at the dinner party, it seems like Lord Quinton forcing her to be paired up with Mr. St. George benefited them both."

"At least you aren't disappointed by the match."

"I'm not. There's someone better waiting for me."

"Well, it'd be nice if he would step forward. I know we have more time in the Season, but a few gentlemen I know have already secured husbands for their sisters and daughters."

She'd like for her admirer to make himself known this evening, but that was hard to do when the poor man was too scared to do so. "I am glad you're allowing me to pick someone I want rather than arranging a marriage for me."

He offered her a smile. "Fortunately, we're in a financial position where I can do that. A lifetime is a long time to spend with someone. It's best if it's someone you can enjoy being with." He scanned the room. "Are you sure you don't want to at least give Lord Wright a chance?"

"I'm sure, Horatio."

"Well, there must be someone I can have you dance with this evening."

"Is there anyone who seems to be looking at me?" She scanned the room with him, but it didn't seem like anyone was paying attention to her except for Edwin.

A gentleman went over to him, and Edwin hurried to fill his glass with wine.

"I don't notice anyone looking over here," Horatio said. "What do you think of that gentleman over there?"

She followed the direction he pointed to. The gentleman was talking to another gentleman. While he seemed to be having a wonderful time, he didn't give an indication that he knew she was in the room. Surely, that could not be her secret admirer. "I don't know."

"You have to dance with someone. Even your friends are dancing."

"All right, I'll dance with him."

As he went over to talk to the gentleman, her gaze swept the room once more. There were a lot of people in attendance. She supposed it would be easy for her admirer to be looking at her without her realizing it. She let out a frustrated sigh. She didn't know why she thought figuring out this mystery would be simple. It was turning out to be far more complicated than she'd imagined.

She glanced over at Edwin. He happened to be looking at her again. That was odd, wasn't it? Of all the people in the room, why was it him who kept looking at her?

As soon as the thought came to her, she dismissed it. She had asked for his help this evening. Certainly, that meant he wouldn't just be watching to see if any gentlemen were particularly interested in her. He would be keeping track of where she was in the room, too. So really, the fact that he was paying attention to her was to be expected. Her brother returned to her with the gentleman. Forcing her mind off of Edwin, she turned to the gentleman and got ready for the next dance.

EDWIN DIDN'T THINK he could be more on edge than he'd been at the dinner party, but every time his master brought over another gentleman to dance with Lady Rachel, the knot in his gut grew tighter. He had to remember his place. He was a butler. He could never be with her. He could be with a maid, perhaps, but a lady of nobility was forbidden to him.

If only I could tell my heart that.

He rolled his eyes. As if his heart would listen.

"What was that?" a lady asked from across the table.

His attention went to the plump middle-aged lady who was among the wealthier households. "Pardon me, my lady?"

"I don't appreciate having someone roll their eyes at me." She scanned him up and down in a dismissive manner. "Especially not one who is a servant."

He stiffened. It could very well put his job in jeopardy if he didn't resolve this matter at once. "I assure you, my lady, that I wasn't doing that at you. My mind wandered and a certain thought came up." He cleared his throat. She didn't need to know the details. No one needed to know the details. "It had to do with an argument between two other servants in the household. It was a frivolous thing. I apologize for letting such a thing interfere with my work here this evening."

The lady relented. "All right. Just make sure you keep your focus where it needs to be. Not everyone is as forgiving as I am." She turned away from the table and headed over to a group of ladies.

He breathed a sigh of relief. That was close. He wiped his forehead then turned his attention back to the wine. Another bottle was empty. He picked up another one and opened it.

SECRET ADMIRER

Without thinking, he searched for Lady Rachel. He didn't realize being at a ball with her in attendance was going to be so difficult. No matter how much he tried, he couldn't seem to stop looking at her.

She was dancing again. She laughed at something the gentleman told her. What he wouldn't give to have the pleasure of hearing her laugh from something witty he told her.

I'm doomed. I'll have to spend the rest of my life loving her from afar. There's just no helping it.

He glanced around the room but didn't see any other gentleman, besides her brother, looking her way. He didn't know what to tell her about this evening. She was bound to ask him if he thought anyone here was her admirer. What was he supposed to tell her? No? Yes? He had no idea? He took a deep breath and released it. He had no idea a single missive could turn into such a complicated thing.

Chapter Seven

"What kind of things interest you?" Lord Swenson asked as Rachel danced with him. "I already bored you with the lectures I've heard on how the Greeks and Romans influenced the construction of modern architecture. It would be in bad form if you collapsed to the floor because you fell asleep. We need to discuss something that will keep you awake."

She chuckled at his joke. "I didn't find the topic boring."

He raised an eyebrow and grinned. "Are you sure? I started telling it to my mother during dinner, and the next thing I know, she started snoring."

"Oh, she did not. Not during dinner."

"She most certainly did. Fortunately, the butler was there to hold her head up. Otherwise, she would have had custard all over her face."

She laughed. She had no idea anyone could have such a marvelous sense of humor. Even if he was exaggerating, she enjoyed the tall tale.

"But seriously, I do want to know something about you. Tell me something about yourself."

Her face flushed, and she wasn't sure if it was from the way he smiled at her or the fact that he seemed interested in her. "I'm afraid there isn't much to say. I don't lead a very interesting life." As soon as she'd said those words, she wished she hadn't. Now she would seem uninteresting. Or, worse, pathetic.

"I find that hard to believe. A pretty lady like you certainly has something fun to tell. Whatever you have to share will be far more interesting than the way buildings are constructed."

After a moment, she came up with something that might be somewhat entertaining. "I'm good at calligraphy. I write letters and designs that my brother likes to have on his stationary."

"I purchased some stationary in the past that had fancy letters on it, but I didn't know the person who drew them. I don't suppose your brother takes your work and sells them to a merchant?"

She shook her head. "I only do it for him."

"I wonder if you're as good as the stationary I purchased. Mind if I come by to see your work sometime?"

Rachel had to stop herself from tripping. Had he just asked if he could pay her a visit? No gentleman had done that before. Lord Swenson could very well be her secret admirer! Perhaps her brother arranging the dance had been the nudge he'd needed to finally talk to her.

Doing her best to keep calm, she said, "I would be delighted to show you my brother's stationary."

"Splendid. I look forward to seeing you again. I'll send a card."

The dance ended, and he gave her a smile that made her heart give an unexpected flutter. She returned his smile then glanced over at Edwin, thinking he would give her a nod to let her know that she'd just danced with her secret admirer, but instead of nodding, she detected something else in his expression. She wasn't sure what it meant. All she knew was that it was a mixture of worry and resignation.

Lydia led Rachel away from the dancing area to where Carol was. "Who was that?" she asked Rachel once they were safely away from the others.

"Lord Swenson," Rachel told her friends. "I think he's my secret admirer."

"What did he say to make you think that?" Carol asked.

SECRET ADMIRER

"He didn't come out and say he is my admirer," Rachel clarified. "But we had a wonderful conversation, and he asked if he could pay me a visit."

Carol's eyes widened in interest. "He did?"

Rachel gave them an excited nod. "No one has asked to visit me before. He's the only one. That has to mean it's him."

"Not necessarily," Lydia said. "This could be someone else who's taken an interest in you."

Rachel shook her head. "That can't be. There's been no one else who's expressed an interest in me all Season."

Lydia rubbed her chin in a thoughtful manner. "Lord Swenson seems rather outgoing to me. I think someone who sends an anonymous love letter is going to be shy."

"I think it could be someone who is shy," Carol began, "or it could be someone who knows her brother wouldn't approve of the match."

Rachel frowned in disappointment. "So neither of you think Lord Swenson could be the gentleman who sent me that wonderful missive?"

"He could be," Lydia assured her. "But I think it's likely to be someone else. I mean, look at him." She gestured to where Lord Swenson was talking with a couple of gentlemen. "He's leading the conversation."

"That's with a group of gentlemen," Rachel pointed out.

"Yes, that's true," Lydia began, "but he's not the least bit shy."

"Nor would your brother forbid the match, would he?" Carol added. "It's not like he's been banned from Lord and Lady Cadwalader's balls."

Rachel took another good look around the room. Not a single gentleman seemed to be paying her any attention. Only Edwin bothered to glance in her direction. She sighed. She really wanted her secret admirer. She didn't think she could enjoy being with someone as much as she would enjoy being with her admirer. Her admirer had the heart of a romantic.

But it could be Lord Swenson. Just because her friends didn't think so, it didn't mean they were right. Her admirer obviously cared very much for her. He couldn't hide his feelings forever. Sooner or later, he'd let something slip that let her know he was the one who sent the missive. It was just a matter of paying careful attention to what the gentlemen around her were saying.

"I notice Lord Quinton isn't here this evening," Lydia said.

Surprised by her friend's disappointment, Rachel asked, "You want to see him again?"

Carol's eyes widened in interest. "What's wrong with him?"

"Everything," Rachel told her. "He's not happy no matter what you do. All he did was complain at my brother's dinner party. He didn't like the color of Miss Carnel's cameo, so he demanded to be paired up with a different lady. The soup was too hot, so he had to wait for it to cool. Then he had Cook list all of the ingredients he used in the meal. And when it came time for playing games, he refused to play charades lest someone unknowingly pretend to be something ominous." Rachel still had no idea what ominous things he expected someone to use in charades. "We ended up playing cards, but he had to sit far enough from Miss Carnel so that he didn't have to see her cameo." She shook her head. "Horatio and I were both relieved when the dinner party was over. The whole evening was ruined because of him."

"That does sound terrible," Carol said.

"It wasn't terrible," Lydia argued. "He's was only a little fearful. We all have things we worry about."

"While we do, he takes it way too far," Rachel replied. "I don't know why anyone would put up with him."

"I know he was difficult, but you could tell he wasn't trying to be that way, couldn't you?" Lydia asked. "He was only trying to protect himself."

Rachel couldn't believe what she was hearing. "Protect himself from what?"

SECRET ADMIRER

Lydia shrugged. "Bad luck, I suppose."

"What bad thing could happen to him at a dinner party?" Rachel asked.

"Maybe he wasn't worried about the dinner party," Lydia began. "Maybe he worried about what would happen when he got home. He mentioned not wanting to have nightmares because of what he was eating. I really don't think he intended to upset anyone. He did apologize to Miss Carnel for inconveniencing her."

Rachel stared at her friend for a long moment then decided it was pointless in reasoning with her friend. If Lydia thought Lord Quinton's actions were acceptable for polite society, that was her problem. As long as Rachel didn't have to deal with him, she was happy.

"I'd rather have someone like Lord Quinton than the gentleman I'm betrothed to," Carol spoke up. "A lady can forgive someone who is scared of bad luck. Being with someone who resents you is another matter."

Rachel and Lydia turned their sympathetic gazes to their friend. When Carol put it like that, Rachel supposed Lord Quinton wasn't that bad.

"Why does your butler keep looking over here?" Lydia asked Rachel.

Surprised by the question, Rachel glanced Edwin's way and saw him quickly avert his gaze. "I asked him to help me figure out who my secret admirer is. That's why my brother is hosting this ball. It allows Edwin to see if there's any gentleman here who seems to be interested in me. But you two can't let anyone else know about it. Even my brother doesn't know."

"We can keep a secret," Lydia assured her. "Though it's odd that he's looking this way when he should be scanning the room to see if a gentleman is paying attention to you, isn't it?"

Carol's gaze swept the room. "Maybe the secret admirer isn't here. I don't see any of the guests looking this way."

Rachel hid her apprehension. It was possible her secret admirer wasn't at this ball. Besides Lord Swenson, she'd had no promising encounters with any of the gentlemen here this evening.

Lydia chuckled.

"What's so funny?" Carol asked before Rachel could.

"Wouldn't it be funny if the secret admirer was the butler?" Lydia asked them. "That would mean the very person who's supposed to be looking for the secret admirer is the secret admirer himself."

"Oh, don't be silly," Rachel replied. "It's not Edwin. Edwin doesn't think of me that way. He's only helping me out because I asked him to. He's doing this out of respect for my brother."

"What does your brother have to do with this?"

"Edwin works for my brother. Our father made him the butler because Edwin did a fine job of taking care of things. I'm sure that Edwin was pleased when he was allowed to be the butler despite being so young. My brother kept him on as the butler when he assumed the title. That's why he's doing this. He's doing this out of respect for my brother."

"If you say so," Lydia replied with a shrug.

In an effort to change the topic, Rachel said, "I thought Mr. St. George was my secret admirer, but he's having his second dance with Miss Carnel, and it's apparent he's interested in her." Since Carol hadn't been at the dinner party, she pointed to the couple so that Carol would know who Mr. St. George and Miss Carnel were.

"I could have told you that Mr. St. George wasn't your secret admirer," Lydia said.

"How? I barely spoke to him during the dinner party," Rachel replied.

Lydia smirked. "Because he didn't look at you the way the butler is."

Rachel rolled her eyes. "That's enough, Lydia. It's not Edwin. Only a gentleman of my social standing would send me that missive. Now, can we talk about something else?"

SECRET ADMIRER

"All right. I'll be good." Lydia turned to Carol. "It's a shame you're betrothed. Otherwise, I'd recommend you meet Lord Wright. He's Miss Carnel's brother. He's recently widowed and looking for a wife to be a mother to his child."

"Your betrothal was the only reason I didn't invite you to the dinner party," Rachel spoke up. "I thought Lord Wright and Lydia would make a good match." She found Lord Wright not too far from his sister. He was talking to a couple of gentlemen. "That's him," she told Carol.

"I wonder if Lord Quinton didn't come because they're here," Lydia said.

"I don't care why Lord Quinton didn't come here this evening," Rachel replied. "I'm just glad he didn't come."

"That's a terrible thing to say, Rachel."

"I mean it, Lydia. He was rude. My brother doesn't want to him around any more than I do. Lord Wright and Miss Carnel probably wouldn't be here this evening if he showed up. I don't understand why you're so nice to Lord Quinton. You'd be much better off with Lord Wright."

"Lord Wright is fine. His money is nice. But Lord Quinton has money, too, and, to be honest, I think Lord Quinton is more attractive."

"He's more attractive than Lord Wright?" Carol asked. "Lord Wright is considerably handsome. If I wasn't betrothed, I would have been happy to let him escort me to dinner." She paused. "I think Lord Wright looks a little uncomfortable, but that's a lot more manageable than being with someone who's angry."

Was Lord Wright uncomfortable? Rachel took a good look at him. She supposed he did look a little reserved. His posture wasn't as relaxed as the other gentlemen's were. He happened to glance their way, and when he realized they were staring at him, he offered a tentative smile as if to greet them.

Face warm, Rachel joined her friends and returned the smile before they took their gazes off of him.

"Maybe he's your secret admirer," Carol said.

"No, it can't be him," Rachel replied as he turned his attention back to the gentlemen he was talking to. "I didn't even meet him until my brother's dinner party. I received that missive before then."

"Maybe he knew who you were before the dinner party," Carol suggested.

"But the gentleman who wrote that missive had talked to me before the dinner party," Rachel said.

Lydia's eyebrow rose. "Are you sure? I don't recall anything in that missive mentioning a conversation you two shared."

Rachel shook her head. "He had to have talked to me before then. How else would he feel so deeply for me?"

"Hmm…" Lydia glanced at Carol. "She has a point. It did sound like he knew a lot about her from what he wrote in that missive."

"To be fair, he didn't write that much," Carol argued. "All he said was that there is no lady lovelier than Rachel. That could refer to her beauty." Her gaze went to Rachel. "You are a beautiful lady."

Lydia gave a thoughtful nod. "When you put it that way, I suppose this admirer didn't have to actually talk to her to be smitten by her."

"But he added that I was kind and that he would forever and always be my admirer," Rachel spoke up. "How can someone write all of that if he doesn't know something about me other than how I look?"

Lydia groaned. "I don't know. Maybe he has talked to you. Maybe he hasn't. All we know is that someone in London is in love with you. Isn't that enough of a reason to be happy?"

"I am happy about it," Rachel said. "I just want to know who he is so I can spend time with him. I'd like to get to know him better. He could very well be my love match." Without thinking, her gaze went to Edwin.

SECRET ADMIRER

Edwin was opening another bottle of wine as the maid set more glasses on the table. Rachel hoped he was able to pick out more than she had during this ball because she didn't think she was getting anywhere, unless Lord Swenson happened to be her admirer.

Sighing, she turned back to her friends as they went on to discuss the latest fashion. Rachel was going to find out who her admirer was. One way or another, she was going to do it. She didn't want to marry someone who only felt a mild affection for her; she wanted to marry someone who was completely devoted to her. Such a husband, she knew, would be perfect.

Chapter Eight

Edwin knew Lady Rachel was eager to talk to him about her secret admirer, but he held off on talking to her for as long as he could. If he told her none of the gentlemen who were guests at the ball were her admirer, she would be disappointed. If he told her someone there was her admirer, she'd want to know who he was, and that would lead to all sorts of problems. He couldn't come out and admit it was him. He didn't know what to do. He couldn't very well make someone up, could he?

Fortunately, he'd been too busy to talk to her right after the ball. Then, the next morning, His Grace kept her distracted as soon as she came downstairs so she didn't have a chance to ask Edwin about the previous evening. And since her brother kept talking, Edwin was able to stay safely to the side of the room while they ate.

"We should ride horses at Hyde Park," His Grace told Lady Rachel as Edwin poured water into his glass. "Perhaps we'll come across a couple of bachelors who choose not to attend balls. Not everyone enjoys them. Some even consider them to be a waste of time."

Lady Rachel glanced at Edwin, but he pretended not to notice as he poured water into her glass. "What time do you want to ride horses?" she asked her brother. "It won't be this morning, will it?"

Edwin resisted the urge to flinch as he returned to his master's side. There was no doubt she was hoping he'd give her good news. Once again, he criticized himself for acting so foolishly. He never should have written that missive. All he'd done was dig himself into a hole he couldn't escape.

"No," her brother assured her. "The notable people of society won't be out until later."

She relaxed and poked her fork into her waffle. "In that case, a horse ride sounds like fun."

Her brother eyed her in interest. "Do you plan to see your friends this morning?"

"Well, no," she slowly replied after she swallowed her food. "I just wanted to enjoy the morning. We've been doing a lot since the Season started."

Her brother offered her an apologetic smile. "I know I've been taking you to a lot of places. You've hardly had time to yourself. But when you secure a marriage to someone you love, it'll be worth it. You only have one Season. You can do whatever you want for the rest of your life."

"Yes, I know."

"I was going to take you to the theatre tomorrow evening. I thought it might be nice to see who is there. If all of the activity has overwhelmed you, however, I suppose it would be better to let you spend the evening here. That is, unless you want to change your mind about going to Carol's dinner party this evening?"

"No, I'm not changing my mind on that. Carol asked me to come. She's nervous about how things will go with her betrothed. Lydia and I want to be there to help ease her nerves." She arched an eyebrow but grinned. "You're not trying to get out of escorting Lydia to dinner this evening, are you?"

Her brother returned the smile. "I made a promise, and I'll follow through with it. Lydia does understand that I have no romantic interest in her, doesn't she? I'm only doing this as a favor to you."

"I think Lydia's as interested in you as you are in her. In fact, I suspect she's entertaining affections for Lord Quinton."

SECRET ADMIRER

Edwin's eyes widened, but it was His Grace who asked, "The same gentleman who was rude at our dinner party?"

Lady Rachel shrugged. "I don't understand it, either. Though to be fair, she doesn't think he was rude. She thinks he was scared."

"Scared of what? A silly cameo and some food?"

"As I said, I don't understand it, Horatio. All I know is that she was hoping to see him last evening at our ball."

"Oh, you're jesting!"

She chuckled. "I assure you that I'm not. She was quite disappointed when she saw he wasn't there."

"I'm glad he didn't show up." He poked the egg with his fork. "I'm hoping to have Lord Wright here for another dinner party. He knows a lot about the financial world. It's nice to have someone I can talk to about money. If he's any good at chess, he might even turn into a friend."

The conversation went on from there, and after His Grace and Lady Rachel were done, Edwin made sure the dishes were removed. The bell in his room rang just as he was putting the silverware away. He glanced at it. That was a summons to the drawing room. No doubt, Lady Rachel was waiting for him under the pretense of wanting tea.

He let out a long sigh. He had put this off for as long as he could. It was time to face the situation. He was just going to have to come out and confess that he had written the missive. He couldn't go on lying to her. It wasn't fair to her. Maybe if he assured her that she really was lovely and, because of that loveliness, she was bound to get a good suitor, she would forgive him.

He finished putting the rest of the silverware away and hurried to get the tea. Black with lemon and some sugar, just as she liked it. Picking up the tray, he took a deep breath. He could do this. As long as she forgave him, his job was secure. He just needed to be mindful of the way he phrased things. He wouldn't act in haste like he had with the missive. He had learned his lesson.

When he arrived at the drawing room, she was pacing in front of the windows. She didn't hide her excitement as he set the tray on the table in front of the settee.

She hurried over to him. "I thought breakfast was never going to end. Sometimes my brother can talk and talk. They say ladies don't know how to be quiet, but those people never met my brother."

He wouldn't mind it if her brother was here right now. It would help if someone would stop this conversation from happening. And that was ironic considering how many times he'd dreamt of what it would be like to have her undivided attention. He poured tea into her cup. Gathering his courage, he straightened up and faced her.

He got ready to speak when she asked, "It's Lord Swenson, isn't it?"

His eyebrows furrowed. "Pardon?"

"Lord Swenson is my secret admirer, isn't he? We danced two times. He was very complimentary, and he even expressed an interest in paying me a visit."

Edwin forced his expression to remain neutral, which was a considerable feat considering how much this news upset him. Yes, he'd seen her dance with quite a few gentlemen last night, and he had worried each and every one would appeal to her. He'd also secretly hoped she'd have no desire to be with any of them. But that was all a fantasy in his mind.

He released his breath then cleared his throat. "You say that Lord Swenson asked to pay you a visit?"

She nodded. "And he was very nice to me. He didn't say things exactly the way he wrote them in the missive, but he let me know he found me to his liking. No other gentleman did that the entire evening. I can't think of anyone else my secret admirer could be. It has to be Lord Swenson. You were there watching me. Didn't Lord Swenson seem like he could be my admirer?"

Well, if Lord Swenson had done all of that, he could very well be her secret admirer. Granted, he wasn't. Edwin was the one who wrote the missive. But now he didn't have to let her know that. He could let her think Lord Swenson wrote it. And if things didn't work out between them, she'd be disappointed but she'd assume they had figured out the mystery. But if things did work out, if she ended up marrying him and having his children, then...then... Edwin fidgeted. He didn't even want to think about it.

"I can't say it's him," Edwin finally said. "The missive was from an anonymous sender."

"Oh, I know that we can't know for sure unless Lord Swenson confesses to writing it. I just think there's a good chance it's him."

When he realized she expected him to respond, he forced out, "If it seems like Lord Swenson has taken an interest in you, then it doesn't matter if he wrote the missive or not, does it? The important thing is that he wants to be your suitor."

She considered his words for a moment then nodded. "I hadn't thought of it that way, but you're right. I hope he is the sender of that missive. It would be romantic if I ended up marrying my secret admirer, but I realize I can't get so attached to the dream of being with my secret admirer that I miss out on a love match. If this admirer is too shy to ever come out and tell me he wants to be with me, there's nothing I can do about it." She turned to the tea. "Why don't you share some tea with me?"

His eyes grew wide. "I can't. I'm the butler."

"It's just a cup of tea. I have no one else to drink this with, and I don't want it to go to waste. Besides, you've been a big help to me. I ought to properly thank you."

The offer was tempting. He would like to sit and talk to her. Perhaps they might even discuss something other than the missive. But did he dare? He glanced at the doorway as if her brother would be standing there with a disapproving frown on his face.

She touched his arm, and he spun back to face her. She'd never touched him before. His body sparked with pleasure.

She retrieved the other cup and poured tea into it. "I mean it. Sit and have some tea with me. No one will mind."

"I'm sure someone would. I don't recall your father or your brother sitting with a servant."

"Maybe not, but they never shared a secret like we do. That makes you more than a servant. You're a friend." She patted the chair next to hers and sat down. "We won't even sit on the settee. There's nothing wrong with two friends sitting in some chairs enjoying tea."

Despite his better judgment, he found himself taking a seat. His heart raced with excitement. Even if this wasn't socially acceptable, he so very much wanted to be near her. Not knowing what to say, he drank some tea.

She smiled after taking a sip. "It's perfect." When he looked at her, she added, "The tea. I didn't think about it before, but it just occurred to me that you always make sure the tea is exactly the way I like it. Thank you."

Face warm, he shrugged. "It's just tea."

"It's more than that. I hadn't considered everything you've done around here, but I should have. I remember my father saying he made you the butler despite your young age because you were the most diligent servant he'd ever had."

Her father had said that about him? Touched, he said, "Your father was a good gentleman. It was an honor to work in his household. Not many servants are as lucky as I was."

"It's no wonder he liked you. My brother does, too. He wouldn't have any other butler." She took another sip of her tea. "Is it hard to be a butler?"

Surprised by the question, he repeated, "Is it hard to be a butler?"

She chuckled. "I know it's a silly question, but I don't know anything about being a butler. I mean, I know you bring the tea and oversee the meals. But what else do you do around here?"

"Oh, well, I make sure there's adequate lighting in the rooms, I make sure the fireplace is roaring when it's cold, I bring the guests who attend dinner parties to this room, I take care of the china, I polish the silverware, I announce when meals are ready, I see to it that the footman and errand boy are ready for their duties, and I make sure the stock of wine is in good order."

Her eyes grew wide. "I had no idea you did so much."

"It's not that much once you get into the routine. Most of the time, everything goes so smoothly that I have plenty of free time to do whatever I want."

"I don't know. I'm quite impressed with that list. I don't make it a habit of doing that much. I usually visit with friends or read a book. Though I will say that ever since my Season started, things have been busy. It seems like I'm always running off to a ball or some other social event." She gave a playful roll of her eyes. "Right now, everything is about finding a husband."

He glanced at the doorway again. Should she be telling him all of this? It wasn't his business what she did or didn't do.

"I don't suppose servants have anything comparable to a Season when they look for someone to marry, do they?" she asked.

He turned his attention back to her. "No, servants don't have Seasons."

"Then how do you find someone to marry?"

"We just happen to find someone who appeals to us, and we marry them." He shrugged. "There's not much to it."

"Are marriages ever arranged for servants?"

"I don't recall that happening for servants. I think it only happens to those of nobility. Well, another butler did tell me about an untitled gentleman who arranged for his son to marry a noble lady. I suppose if one has enough wealth, it doesn't matter if they are of nobility or not."

She nodded in a thoughtful fashion which only seemed to enhance her beauty. He shifted uncomfortably in the chair. It wasn't right for him to look at her with such longing. If someone happened to see them, they would know how he felt about her. He forced his gaze back to his cup and took another drink.

"My brother has allowed me the freedom to choose the gentleman I will marry," she said. "I'm fortunate that way, but I confess that it makes it difficult, too."

His eyebrows furrowed. "How so?"

"I had to go into the Season not knowing if I'll marry or not. A lady has a lot of pressure to marry her first Season. If she has a second Season, it's all right, though not ideal. If she doesn't marry in her third Season, then she's thought to be undesirable."

Now he better understood why she worried no gentleman would take an interest in her. He doubted her brother had to worry about how many years it would take him to get married.

"Are you in love with anyone?" she asked.

He turned his wide eyes in her direction, surprised she'd ask the question.

"I won't tell anyone if you are," she continued, keeping her voice low.

It took him a long moment to come up with a reply. "I don't think I'm in the position to answer that question. I'm only a butler. This is something you should ask someone equal to you."

"Oh, I suppose you're right. It probably is inappropriate. I'm sorry. I meant no harm in it."

Relaxing, he smiled. "It's all right."

"I hope you don't mind that I wanted to talk to you. There's something about you that makes me feel comfortable. Maybe it's because you don't have any expectations of me. I don't have to be a noble lady. I can just be me."

"How is being a noble lady difficult?"

"When you deal with certain people, you're expected to be confident all the time. You're not allowed to question yourself."

SECRET ADMIRER

"You question yourself?"

"Not often, but sometimes I do. I wonder if I say the right thing or if I look suitable for a certain social activity. London is a big place, but people seem to know what you're doing any time you leave the townhouse. You wouldn't believe how fast a rumor can spread. If you do the slightest thing to upset an influential member of the Ton, you might as well escape to the country and live out the rest of your life there. Even if I do manage to find a husband this Season, I'll still have rumors to worry about." She paused. "I don't suppose servants feel pressure to meet anyone's expectations, do they?"

"If we don't do things as our masters expect, we can lose our jobs. That's worrisome."

She leaned toward him. "Is it?"

He tried hard not to notice her cleavage. Her movement had been innocent, but it had also allowed him to see the top of her breasts. He forced his gaze to her face. "I don't want to be without a roof over my head or food on my plate. Without this job, I have nothing."

His gaze went back to her cleavage, and his face warmed in embarrassment. He didn't know if he'd ever be able to get that vision out of his mind. Not that he wanted to, but he had to try. He had no right to enjoy the view, and what was more, if he kept thinking about it, it was going to be hard to sleep tonight.

He brought the cup to his mouth to drink more tea, but it was empty. He set the cup on the tray and took a deep breath. It wasn't safe to stand up yet. His erection was too strong. He had to get rid of it before he could leave the room. He looked back at the doorway, praying no one, especially not her brother, was going to show up.

"You have nothing to worry about," Lady Rachel said.

He looked at her in surprise. She didn't notice how attracted he was to her, did she?

She leaned back and smiled. "Your job is secure at this townhouse. I can't imagine a reason why my brother would ever relieve you of your duties."

He could, but he didn't dare tell her that. At least he could no longer see so much of her breasts that it was distracting him. Maybe now his erection would go away. He took a deep breath and released it.

To his dismay, she leaned forward again, but this time she also touched his arm. "I'm glad I could reassure you."

He heard footsteps and shot a frantic gaze to the doorway. She jumped up from the chair and ran to the door just in time for her brother to pop into view. He whispered a quick prayer to will his erection away. God help him if her brother noticed it! She might be oblivious to it, but her brother certainly wouldn't be.

"I think I might have a suitor," she told her brother before her brother glanced in Edwin's direction. "Lord Swenson mentioned paying me a visit sometime."

"Why didn't you mention this earlier?" her brother asked. "Don't tell me a missive arrived this early in the day."

"No, nothing arrived. I wasn't even sure I should say something until a missive arrived."

"Well, if he does come here, I'll be happy to chaperone the visit."

Thankfully, Edwin's erection finally went away. He hurried to stand up and picked up the tray before his master noticed that he had been having tea with his sister. He quietly passed them and headed down the hall.

He breathed a sigh of relief. His master hadn't even glanced his way. Once again, being a servant had worked to his advantage. It had made him invisible to the nobility around him. He couldn't bring himself to interact with his master. Not now. He needed some time to settle his nerves.

He'd not only been physically aroused by Lady Rachel, but he'd been emotionally excited, too. Up to day, he hadn't ever had an actual conversation with her where she'd spoken so casually with him. She was even kinder than he'd thought. Yes, she would make someone a wonderful wife. The day she announced the gentleman she'd be marrying was going to be the worst day of his life.

Chapter Nine

"Thank you for coming," Carol whispered to Rachel and Lydia that evening after they arrived at the dinner party. "I don't know what I'd do if you couldn't make it."

Rachel glanced over at the Duke of Augustine as he talked with Horatio and Carol's forty-year-old uncle, the Duke of Havre, who was her guardian. Most of the time, Carol came to Rachel's townhouse to visit. She never said much about her uncle, and all Rachel had ever done was offer a polite greeting if they happened to meet in public. Judging by the bored expression on his face, it was apparent that he didn't want to be here this evening. The Duke of Augustine didn't look bored, though there was something about him that told Rachel he didn't want to be here, either.

Rachel thought the dinner party at her residence had been awkward, but this was bound to be worse. She glanced at the butler who frowned when he noticed she was looking at him. She quickly looked away. He wasn't Edwin. Edwin never frowned at her. He always smiled. It was startling how different butlers could be.

"The wedding is in a month," Carol whispered. "The closer the day comes, the worse I feel." She clutched her stomach. "I wish I could get out of it."

Lydia put her hand on her shoulder and squeezed it. "I'm sorry, Carol. I wish there was something I could do."

"We both wish we could do something," Rachel added.

"I know." Carol wiped her eyes. "You two are the only ones who understand what I'm going through. No one else cares. I tried to talk my uncle into letting me out of the marriage agreement, but he won't do it. He wants to get rid of me, and this is the easiest way he can do it."

Lydia's eyebrows furrowed. "Did he say he wanted to get rid of you?"

"He doesn't need to," Carol said. "Ever since he inherited my father's title, he's been wanting this townhouse all to himself. The Duke of Augustine isn't any better. Both of them act like I'm an inconvenience to them."

Rachel bit her lower lip. She had noticed that the two gentlemen were talking on the other side of the room when she'd arrived with Lydia and Horatio. They had greeted the new arrivals, but they'd only invited Horatio to talk with them.

"It's a shame you're not my sister," Rachel told Carol. "Horatio would never make you marry His Grace. He would find a way to annul the agreement."

"It would be nice if I was your sister," Carol replied. "You're fortunate your brother cares about what you want."

Rachel did consider herself fortunate. She happened to be under the care of a gentleman who was allowing her a love match.

"Do you want to run off to my family's estate?" Lydia asked Carol in a low voice.

"I can't do that," Carol replied. "Your family doesn't have any money. I'd be a burden to you."

"We'll have money as soon as I manage to marry a wealthy gentleman," Lydia said.

Rachel grimaced. "I hope you're not thinking of marrying Lord Quinton."

Lydia gave her a pointed look. "Why not? He showed an interest in me at your dinner party."

"He was interested in the color of your hair and the color of your gown," Rachel argued. "If you had been wearing a peacock cameo and a red gown, he would have chosen someone else."

"There was more to it than those things," Lydia insisted. "He was looking at me in a way that made me feel all nice and warm inside. No one has ever looked at me that way before."

Rachel inwardly groaned but decided to end the argument. She didn't know what it was about Lord Quinton that was attractive to her friend. She just hoped her friend wasn't going to end up doing something foolish. Hopefully, her friend would have better offers during this Season. Then she could put Lord Quinton behind her.

The butler announced that dinner was ready. Horatio was the first one to make his way over to them. He took Lydia's arm. Rachel accepted the Duke of Havre's arm, though she couldn't bring herself to look directly at him. His low sigh was enough to tell her he was anxious for the evening to be over. The Duke of Augustine's jaw clenched as he held his arm out to Carol. Rachel blinked. Carol might be dreading the upcoming marriage, but it was obvious that he resented it. He might even hate her because of it.

The meal was awkward, to say the least. Horatio did most of the talking, and Rachel chimed in as much as she could to keep things pleasant. Lydia would make a comment once in a while, too. The two dukes, however, seemed to have no interest in participating, and Carol kept blinking back tears from her eyes. The servants moved about stiffly, as if they felt like they were walking on egg shells. Rachel wished Edwin was in charge of the dinner instead of the Duke of Havre's butler. Then, at least, she'd feel a bit better. She was so anxious during the meal that she would have welcomed Lord Quinton's ridiculous comments about clothes, food, or nightmares!

Finally, the dinner came to an end, but it led to an equally uncomfortable game of cards. Toward the end of the evening, Horatio had given up on trying to keep up a pleasant conversation going, and Rachel couldn't blame him. She didn't know what Carol was supposed to do. Rachel could get away from this situation when the dinner party was over. Her poor friend was stuck in this for the rest of her life.

Rachel waited until she, Horatio, and Lydia were in the carriage before saying, "Can't we do something to prevent this marriage from happening?"

"Like what?" Horatio asked.

"Something. Anything."

"From what her uncle said, their fathers signed a contract, and that contract is binding."

Rachel glanced at Lydia who shrugged in a way that let her know she was just as baffled as Rachel was. Rachel groaned. "You're a gentleman," she told her brother. "Maybe you can talk to someone who can break the contract."

"Even if I knew someone who could do that," her brother began, "it's not my place to interfere. I'm not related to Carol."

"But you can tell the Duke of Augustine doesn't want to marry her."

He winced. "Yes. It's obvious he doesn't want the match."

"He resents it."

After a moment, he nodded. "That would be a fair assessment of the situation."

"We should just take Carol to my family's estate," Lydia insisted.

"What good would that do when your family's estate is in poor condition?" Rachel asked. "Even if you married a wealthy gentleman, it'll take years to restore that manor to what it used to be." She directed her gaze to Horatio. "We can take Carol to our country estate."

"If we did that, her uncle would consider that abduction, and we would get in trouble," he told her.

"We'd only get in trouble if someone found out what we did," Rachel replied.

He shook his head. "We might not like what's happening, but we can't stop it. She's under twenty-one. Her guardian has every right to make her marry the Duke of Augustine."

How the rules frustrated Rachel at times! "Then ask the Duke of Augustine to release her from that marital arrangement. Surely, since he's over twenty-one and a gentleman, he should be able to do something."

"Not without her guardian's approval, he can't. Her guardian stands in the place of her father. He can do whatever he wants." When Rachel let out a groan, he added, "I don't know her guardian that well, but he has the reputation of being a difficult gentleman. Her father was the same way. I am sorry she's stuck in this situation, but there's nothing I can do about it. The best she can do is live in a separate townhouse from the Duke of Augustine. He has enough money for this, and from the way he talked, I suspect that's what he'll do."

"That means she'll never find a love match."

He turned his tender eyes in her direction. "Not everyone can have the luxury of finding a love match like you do, Rachel. There are plenty of people who don't love each other but marry anyway. I'm afraid your friend is going to be one of them."

The carriage came to a stop. Rachel was too upset to wish Lydia a good night as she left the carriage. Carol had warned her that the Duke of Augustine kept scowling at her, but she hadn't realized things were this bad for her friend until tonight. If only there was something she could do to stop the wedding from taking place.

As the carriage moved forward, her brother put his arm around her. "I know it's not fair."

"Can't you run off to Gretna Green to marry her?"

"She's betrothed."

"So what if she is betrothed? Just run off with her. Elope. You'll be better to her than the duke will be."

"Her uncle would annul the marriage."

"That can't be true."

"Yes, it is. The only thing that would stop the marriage is if the Duke of Augustine dies or disappears, and I don't see either one of those things happening."

"If you run off to another country like America or Canada, no one will find you."

"All of my investments and the family's estate are tied here. I can't just run off and leave London. It's unfortunate that things between Carol and the Duke of Augustine are bad, but you and I are in no position to interfere. The best you can do is be there for her when she needs you."

He was right. As much as she hated it, he was right. The carriage came to a stop, this time in front of their townhouse. Shoulders slumped, she left the carriage and trudged up the steps.

Edwin was there to greet them as they came in. He glanced her way, a spark of sympathy crossing his face when he noted her expression. She lowered her gaze. If she continued to make eye contact with him, she might burst into tears.

"Is there anything I can bring either one of you?" Edwin asked her and her brother.

"Nothing for me, thanks," her brother said. "I'm going to retire to the den and have a drink."

He headed down the hall.

In the past, she would have headed up the stairs to her bedchamber, but something stopped her from doing that tonight.

"Lady Rachel?" Edwin softly asked.

"Can you bring me some tea? I'll be in the drawing room."

He indicated he would get the tea and left.

She took a deep breath and released it. She removed her coat and her hat before she went to the drawing room. Once there, she went to the fireplace. The fire was burning low. It hadn't been burning when she and Horatio left. Edwin had done that while they were gone. She glanced around the room and saw that a few candles were lit. Edwin had done all of this in case she or her brother wanted to come in here after the dinner party. How many things did he do every day that she hadn't bothered to notice before?

She sat in a chair and put her face in her hands. It wasn't fair that there were so many rules people were expected to follow. Marriage was a lifetime commitment. Why should someone be forced to marry another person simply because their fathers signed a contract? There ought to be something that would allow the contract to be null and void if either the lady or the gentleman protested it, and that something shouldn't involve a guardian's permission.

She heard someone enter the room and lifted her head. Edwin set the tray, which held a single cup with the teapot, on the table in front of her.

"Would you like me to add another piece of wood to the fire?" Edwin asked.

"No, I'm fine." When he gave a nod and started to leave, she called out, "Will you stay with me?"

He paused halfway to the door and turned. "Pardon?"

"Will you stay?" She gestured to the chair close by. "You can sit here."

He glanced at the chair then shook his head. "I can't. Speaking to you in the daytime when everyone is awake and walking through this townhouse is one thing, but it's too late to speak with you now."

"I don't want to be alone. Please?"

His gaze went to the doorway before he went over to her and whispered, "It's inappropriate for me to be with you like this, especially at night."

"No one has to know you're here. The drapes are closed." She motioned to the windows. "My brother is in the den, and as you said, the others are asleep. I need to talk to someone right now, and the only person I feel comfortable talking to about this is you."

A flicker of worry crossed his face. "Did something bad happen?"

She nodded. "That's why I need someone to talk to."

He gave another good look at the doorway.

"If you close it, then no one will see you in case they wake up. As for my brother, he can spend hours in the den."

When his gaze went back to her, she folded her hands together and peered up at him. "Please do this for me, Edwin."

He let out a groan, rolled his eyes, and went to close the door. At once, she felt better. There was something about his calming presence that helped to steady her emotions.

He moved the chair so that he was across from her. "This is risky. I hope you know I can't stay here for long. If we're caught like this, things won't go well." He poured tea into her cup.

"If we're caught, all they'll see is you sitting across from me."

"Yes, but they might assume something more is going on."

"I don't see how they can deny what their eyes are showing them."

She realized people didn't make it a habit of sitting and talking to their servants, but she didn't see the harm in it. It wasn't like she was taking him to her bedchamber. If someone caught them in her bedchamber, then she could understand the need to worry. Not that she'd dream of doing such a thing. She wasn't one of those ladies who shared dalliances with gentlemen she wasn't married to.

Ignoring the tentative expression on his face, she said, "I just wanted to talk to someone about my friend. She's being forced to marry a gentleman who doesn't want the marriage any more than she does. There's nothing they can do to get out of the union. Even my brother, with all of his money, can't help her."

Rachel accepted the cup he gave her and forced down a swallow of the tea. "I've never felt more helpless in my entire life. I want to help my friend, but I can't. And that's all because of some rules set by others who have nothing to win or lose by the marriage. Someone decided it was a good idea to set down limits on what a lady and gentleman can do before they're twenty-one. That would be fine if people had to wait until twenty-one to marry, but that's not the case. They want most ladies to marry before they're twenty-one. I understand the age is older for gentlemen, but a contract can still dictate the gentleman's future." When she realized she was talking fast, she stopped and took a deep breath. "I'm sorry. I'm so upset that I can't relax."

"You have no need to apologize," he said. "And it is upsetting when someone doesn't have control over their future, especially when that someone is a person we care about."

She wiped a tear from her eye and took a sip of the tea. Already, she felt some of the tension easing from her. By the way he spoke, she could tell he did understand her frustration. "Do you feel that you have no control over your future?"

"There are some things I'm not permitted to do." He shrugged. "I've come to accept it."

"What do you wish you could do but can't?"

He shifted uncomfortably in the chair. "I'm not complaining. I am happy to be here."

Her eyebrows furrowed as she studied him. There was something he wanted to do but couldn't. Did she have a right to ask what it was, or was it best she not press the issue?

"I wish there was an answer to your friend's problem," he continued. "Unfortunately, there are rules we are all expected to follow. Even if those rules aren't fair, we can't change them."

"Yes, my brother said that in the carriage on the way home."

"It's good this lady has you for a friend. You care very much for people. It's your best quality."

Her gaze met his, and she noted something in his eyes she hadn't realized was there before. She couldn't quite make out what it was, but it flooded her with a pleasant warm feeling. She cleared her throat. "It's easy to care for someone who's my friend." She took another sip of the tea. "I suppose we're all bound by rules of some sort. It's just that some rules are unfair." She hesitated to ask the question, but she had to know the answer. "Edwin, if there was something my brother or I could do to make things better for you, what would that be?"

She wasn't sure why the question should make him uneasy, but he shifted uncomfortably in the chair again. "You and your brother have been very kind to me. I am happy working here."

"So there's nothing we can do to make things better?"

"I have nothing I can ask for."

The answer should have satisfied her, and yet, she sensed he was holding something back from her. "I suppose when you work for a household, there's only so much you're allowed to do. It's all right that you don't tell me everything. It's not my place to pry." She finished her tea then stood up.

He hurried to his feet.

She smiled. "Thank you for spending some time with me when you could have been doing something else. I don't know why, but I feel at ease when I'm with you. I wish I had taken the time to have talked to you like this sooner. You are a wonderful person, Edwin. I hope you know that you're more than a butler in this house." Now that she had relaxed, the exhausting dinner party was finally catching up to her. "I hope you have pleasant dreams."

"I hope you have pleasant dreams, too, Rachel." He blinked then corrected, "I mean, Lady Rachel."

"I don't mind being called Rachel." She smiled again before she left the room.

Chapter Ten

Edwin had no recourse but to pen his feelings on parchment. He'd tried, unsuccessfully, to sleep. The moon was already dipping lower in the night sky. Dawn would be coming within the next two hours. If he had fancied himself in love with Rachel before, he was much more so now. What man could sleep when he was in love?

For the first time in his life, he hated the fact that he hadn't been born in a noble household or, at the very least, in the home of a wealthy middle class gentleman and lady. There was nothing he could bring to a marriage with Rachel. He was only the butler, and while that was a good place to be among the household staff, it wasn't good enough to be her husband.

As she'd said, London had rules. That meant everyone had their place. One couldn't step outside their bounds. Whether right or wrong, everyone was stuck with the position they were born in.

All he could do was write down what he'd tell her if he had the freedom to be her suitor. He didn't leave anything out. Now he understood what had compelled him to write that first missive. It had been more than simply wanting to assure her that she was desirable. It'd been the only way he had been able to let her know that he found her desirable. Except he had kept his identity a secret. That had been a mistake since all it'd done was threaten to expose him. This time, he would be smart about things. He would never show this to her. He would keep this missive in his desk.

The action of writing everything down helped to settle his swirling emotions. Afterward, he managed a couple of hours of sleep before he had to get up and tend to his duties. His master was the first one to come down the stairs. Edwin was always anxious whenever Rachel showed up in the drawing room, and he was even more so this morning.

As of late, she'd taken note of him and smiled when she saw him, but this morning, she walked up to him. "How are you doing today, Edwin?"

Aware that her brother looked up from the paper he'd been reading, Edwin told her, "I'm doing fine, Lady Rachel. And you?"

"All things considered, I'm all right." She glanced at the tea. "Thank you for bringing tea in here."

"I was only doing my job."

"I know, but you always put a hint of lemon in my cup, and I appreciate that."

Her brother arched an eyebrow.

Edwin gave her a smile to show her he appreciated the compliment. "I better check to see if breakfast is ready." Then he hurried out of the room before he got in trouble with her brother for talking to her.

AS RACHEL TOOK A SIP of her tea, her brother set his paper on his lap and leaned toward her. "Why are you speaking so intimately with the butler?"

"I wasn't speaking intimately with him. I only said hello and thanked him for the tea."

"You went directly over to him and made an attempt to open a conversation with him. You never did that before."

She wasn't sure what he expected her to say, but she saw no reason to lie. "It turns out Edwin is a kind person. I figure it would be a good idea to let him know I appreciate his friendship."

He blinked. "Friendship? What friendship?"

SECRET ADMIRER

"He's been good to us all of these years."

"He's the butler. His job is to be good to us. Exactly how did you two become friends?"

She bit her lower lip for a moment then decided she should tell him everything. He was her brother, after all. She put the cup back on the tray and turned to him. "All right. I'll tell you. I have a secret admirer."

His eyes grew wide. "Is the secret admirer the butler?"

"No, of course not. It's one of the gentlemen who happened to notice me but is too afraid to come out and say something. I only enlisted Edwin's help to find out who this gentleman is."

"Why?"

"Because Edwin gave me the missive."

"Because he wrote it."

She rolled her eyes. "Don't be silly. He's not my secret admirer. He received the missive from my secret admirer at the door. A lad brought it, and Edwin gave it to me to read."

"What did this missive say?"

"Oh, Horatio, that's private."

"Did you tell Edwin the contents of it?"

"No, I would never tell him anything so private."

"But you told those two friends of yours, didn't you? You tell Lydia and Carol everything."

Her face warmed. "They happened to be here the day it arrived, so yes, I let them read it."

"If you let them know the contents, why can't you tell me?"

"I don't know. It just feels strange to confide something so personal to my brother."

"You would rather tell Lydia and Carol than me?"

Noting the hurt tone in his voice, she relented. "You're important to me, too, Horatio. You're more than my brother; you're my friend." When he arched an eyebrow, she said, "I'll tell you, but it is a private note. I don't want others to know. This gentleman poured his heart out to me. It must have taken him a lot of courage to do that."

"It would be more courageous if he told you in person so you'd know who he is."

"If you're going to be like that, then I don't want to tell you anything that's in the missive."

He stared at her for a moment then put his hands up in the air. "All right, I'll refrain from questioning this gentleman's courage. What did he say in the missive?"

"He said I was beautiful and kind and that I'm the loveliest lady in London. It was really a wonderful missive. There was a certain tenderness in the note that told me his feelings for me are sincere. I want to find out who he is. I asked Edwin to help me figure out who he is."

"Why would you ask for Edwin's help but not mine?"

"As I said, the missive is private."

"It wasn't too private for the butler to know about it."

"I didn't tell him what the missive said. I only said the missive was from a secret admirer. I figured since he is a butler that he will notice things we'd miss. I asked him to watch the gentlemen at the ball you hosted the other night so he could tell me if one of them seemed like he could be my secret admirer."

His eyes grew wide. "You what?"

She waved for him to calm down. "He was able to do his job while watching the guests. All he did was pour wine all evening."

Horatio paused then shook his head. "I still don't understand why you trusted him with this more than you trusted me. It's not the butler's business what's happening to you."

She didn't know how to answer him. It was natural that he'd wonder why she'd go to Edwin before going to him about the missive. She supposed that she should have gone to him instead. But things just evolved to the point where she felt like going to Edwin instead of him.

SECRET ADMIRER

After a moment, she ventured, "At first, I only wanted to know if Edwin knew who delivered the missive."

"That part makes sense. But why would you ask for his help at the ball?"

That was a good question. She mulled it over in her head, and as she did, she realized there was something about Edwin that made her feel safe. She didn't worry that he would laugh at her about pining over a secret admirer, and he wouldn't think she was silly by trying to figure out who this admirer was.

"Edwin notices things other people miss," she finally said. "Because he is a butler, he can stand to the side of a room and watch people without them picking up on it. Think of it," she continued when her brother didn't seem convinced of her argument. "How many times have you been aware he's in the room?"

Horatio blinked in surprise, and he scanned the room.

She followed his gaze and saw they were alone. "See? If he had been in this room just now, we wouldn't have realized it. His assistance at the ball was valuable, Horatio. At the ball, Lord Swenson expressed an interest in me, and it turns out Edwin noticed it, too. We believe Lord Swenson is my secret admirer."

Horatio frowned. "Lord Swenson?"

She nodded. "He was really funny when we were dancing at the ball."

"But I introduced you two."

"Sure, we hadn't formally met, but he could have been aware of me all of this time. He was probably delighted when you brought him over to me."

Horatio sat back in his chair and studied her for a long moment. "Do you fancy him?"

Her face warmed. "I don't know him well enough to make that confession, but I thought he was charming."

83

He relaxed. "All right. It's good to know you have taken an interest in someone."

"Things look very promising with him." She picked up her cup and took another sip of her tea.

"Next time you get correspondence of a romantic nature, I want to know about it. You're my sister. I want to know what's happening with you."

She gave him a smile. "If I receive another missive from my secret admirer, I'll let you know."

"Thank you. I'd like to think that you'd rather confide in me than the butler." He retrieved his paper and turned back to the article he'd been reading when she came into the room.

She noticed a movement out of the corner of her eye and saw Edwin pass by the doorway. Her skin warmed. She bit her lower lip. Did her skin warm because she and Horatio had been talking about him, or did it warm because she was beginning to realize how nice he was?

She glanced at her brother, afraid he might pick up on the latter reason. She liked talking to Edwin. She didn't want to stop just because he was the butler. It didn't seem fair that she couldn't be friends with someone unless he had a certain social status. Weren't people more than the role they'd been born into? Shouldn't they be appreciated for who they were? Eyebrows furrowed, she continued to drink her tea.

Chapter Eleven

The moment Edwin had been dreading came at one that afternoon. He had been warned the missive was coming. He'd seen the way Lord Swenson had looked at Rachel when they danced at the ball, and she had commented on how well that dance had gone. So it wasn't a surprise when he took Lord Swenson's missive from the footman.

Since it was addressed to Rachel, he went to the drawing room where she was working on her embroidery. She liked to do that from time to time. If she wasn't visiting with her friends or reading a book, she would sew a pretty design on a piece of linen. She mostly sewed flowers, but on this particular day, she was sewing a cat. He tried not to glance at her breasts as he approached, but she was sitting and this allowed him a generous view of her cleavage he otherwise would not be privy to.

When she looked up at him, heat crept up his cheeks. Surely, she couldn't tell he'd been looking at her inappropriately, could she? He cleared his throat. "This came for you, Lady Rachel."

"I told you that you can call me Rachel. Truly, I don't mind." She set her sewing aside and stood up. When she took the missive, her face lit up. "It's from my secret admirer."

He hid back a grimace. Let her think what she wanted. Being a servant, he was in no position to tell her the truth.

"Would you like me to bring you something to eat or drink?" he asked.

"No, I'm fine, thank you."

He offered her a nod and turned to leave.

"Wait." She darted in front of him. "Don't you want to know what he has to say?"

No, he didn't. What good would it do for him to know that Lord Swenson would get the chance to be her suitor? It didn't change anything. He'd still have no chance to be with her. "The missive is addressed to you. It's not addressed to me."

"But you know about the secret admirer, and you've been willing to help me figure out who he is. Don't you want to know if he admits it in this missive?"

"I doubt he'd come out and admit it. If he wanted you to know his identity, he would have told you in the missive he already sent."

"Oh, come on, Edwin. This has been the most exciting thing that's ever happened to me. How many ladies can say they've received such a lovely note?"

He was sure no other butlers were stupid enough to send the lady of the house a lovesick note. "I'd rather not be here when you read the missive."

Before he could take a step forward, she asked, "Did my brother forbid you to be friends with me?"

He didn't hide his surprise. She thought of him as a friend? While it wasn't exactly the kind of relationship he wanted to have with her, he was shocked that she had chosen to think of him so informally. He would have expected her to keep thinking of him as the butler. He cleared his throat. "No, your brother hasn't spoken to me about you."

"Good. I was hoping he wouldn't. I like you, Edwin. I don't think there's any reason why we can't be friends even though you're a butler. It's not what a person does for a living that defines them; it's who the person is. Don't you agree?"

"I think very highly of you, but I'm afraid your brother is right. This is London. Sisters of a duke don't befriend the butler."

"I disagree. Edwin, you are a nice person, and I happen to think you're more than a butler."

He wasn't sure how to respond to that, so he didn't. He just stood in front of her like a fool while she opened the missive. She only meant he was her friend. She did not think of him romantically. No matter how much he might wish it, there could never be anything of a romantic nature between them. When it came to finding a husband, logic would compel her to pick a titled or a wealthy gentleman.

She frowned as she read the missive, and his eyebrows furrowed. "Didn't Lord Swenson ask to see you?"

"Well, yes, he did," she began, "but he isn't as eloquent in his writing as I expected. He doesn't sound like my secret admirer."

"He doesn't?" How could she tell the difference? The missive he had written her wasn't that long. Just what could she have picked up from his words that were different from Lord Swenson's?

"He isn't poetic."

"Poetic?"

"The gentleman who wrote the other missive had a poetic way about him. I think he loves poetry. You can feel his emotion when you read his words." She gestured to the note she was holding. "I don't feel anything when I read Lord Swenson's missive."

"Those are just words on a paper." Really, he didn't see how anyone could *feel* anything by reading them. Though, he had to admit, it was a bit disturbing that she'd made the comment about poetry. Edwin happened to have a few books of poems in his room.

She sighed in disappointment. "I was looking forward to seeing him, but I'm not sure I want to anymore."

While a part of him was relieved to hear this, the more rational part had to argue. "That doesn't make any sense. You said he was nice to you at the ball." He gestured to the missive in her hand. "And he would like to get to know you better."

"Yes, and those are good reasons to see him."

He stared her as he waited for her to continue.

She shrugged. "I don't know how to explain it. He just doesn't sound like my secret admirer. I know it's silly, but I think I've fallen in love with the gentleman who wrote that love note."

"It is silly." Especially since the two of them could never be equal in station. "You're basing everything off of a missive you received weeks ago. That's just one missive. You have a titled gentleman who is seeking your attention. That's more important than a missive sent by some stranger."

"My secret admirer doesn't think of me as a stranger. He loves me."

Edwin's face warmed, and he prayed she didn't notice the telltale sign of the blush on his face. If she did, there would be no hiding the truth from her.

"But I see your point," she continued as she reread Lord Swenson's missive. "I may never find out who this secret admirer is. He might be too shy to ever come to me in person. I can't spend my life pining away for someone I'll never meet. I will tell my brother about this missive, and my brother will arrange for a time for Lord Swenson to visit." He thought that was the end of the conversation, but she added, "Edwin, do butlers ever marry?"

He blinked. "You want to know if butlers ever marry?"

"I know some servants do, but being a butler, you have more duties and responsibilities than some of the other servants do. Do butlers have time for a wife and children?"

"When something is important, you make time for it. I know a couple of butlers who have families of their own."

"But how do butlers meet ladies to marry?"

He thought for a moment. "I suppose they meet them while out of the townhouse running an errand, though I believe sometimes a relationship can start with another member of the staff. I know a footman who fell in love with the chambermaid of a certain household. They were allowed to marry." And that marriage made sense, given that they were both servants.

"Is there anyone you want to marry?"

He shifted from one foot to another. He wished this conversation hadn't taken such a personal turn.

Her eyes lit up. "There is! Who is she? Does she work here?"

Oh dear. This wasn't good. She was too close for comfort. "I can't tell you that. It's not my place."

Though she seemed disappointed, she smiled. "I'm sorry. I didn't mean to make you uncomfortable."

Glad she wasn't going to press him on the issue, he released his breath. That had been close. For a second, he had actually considered telling her the truth. And that would have been a disaster. She'd be forced to remind him that there could never be anything between them because she was the sister of a duke and all he could ever be was a servant in a household.

"I should show this missive to my brother," she said after a long moment of silence passed between them. "I know others consider it strange that you and I get along as well as we do, but I am glad you take the time to talk with me."

She reached out and touched his arm. He was sure she meant to give him a pat, but for some reason, her touch lingered longer than it should have. His body warmed in pleasure. He had to force his expression to remain neutral, lest he give away his feelings. Then she would know exactly who it was he wanted to marry. Her gaze went from his to where her hand was, and he noted the blush that crept up her cheeks before she pulled her hand away from him.

She cleared her throat then gestured to the missive. "I won't keep you from your duties." She smiled again, and this time, there seemed to be an uncertainty in it. Then she hurried out of the room.

He stared after her. No. It was his imagination. He wanted so badly to be with her that he was picking up on things that weren't there. She only saw him as the butler. There was no way she could be romantically attracted to him. No way at all. With a shake of his head, he went to check on the dishes that would be used for dinner that evening.

Chapter Twelve

Rachel's steps slowed as she approached the library. What was wrong with her? Her hands were shaking. And it had nothing to do with Lord Swenson's missive.

She glanced behind her in the hallway. Thankfully, she was alone. She didn't know why, but it seemed important that no one see her right now. She reached the closed door of the library and leaned against the wall to calm the nervous energy coursing through her body.

Something happened back there in the drawing room, though she couldn't make sense of it. She'd been talking to Edwin, just as she'd done at other times. Then she touched him, and... and...

Something happened. She didn't know if it had only happened to her or if it happened to both of them, but something had definitely taken place between them. It'd been the strangest sensation, too. It was if she had been asleep and had just woken up from a long dream. Edwin was the same, and yet, he wasn't.

She took a deep breath and slowly released it in an attempt to calm her racing heart. It only worked a little. Her heart was still beating faster than usual. She put her hand over it. Whatever could she do to get it back to its normal pace?

The door opened, and her brother jerked when he saw her. "Rachel, what is it?"

It took her a moment to remember why she had come to the library. She stepped away from the wall and held the missive to him. "Lord Swenson asked if he could visit me."

Her brother accepted the missive and smiled. "I dare not refuse the visit since you're so excited about it. I've never seen you so flushed before."

Was she flushed? She put her hand to her cheek. She supposed her skin was warmer than normal.

"Should I tell him to come by tomorrow afternoon, or do you want to make him wait for a little bit?" he asked. "We could arrange for him to come in two or three days."

"Oh, um, what do you think is best?"

He tapped the missive against his free hand as he considered their options. "I suppose if it was me, I'd be satisfied with two days. This is the first time you're seeing him in your home. You want to let him know you're interested, but you don't want him to think you're pining away for him. Yes, I think two days will suffice." He turned on his heel and went back into the library.

Rachel didn't know why, but she glanced over her shoulder before following him into the room. She was happy to note that she was beginning to settle down. Talking to her brother had helped make her feel like her normal self.

Her brother went to the desk and pulled out a piece of parchment from the drawer. "I'm relieved someone is taking an interest in you. For the life of me, I can't imagine why no one has asked to visit you until now."

"There is someone who has expressed his interest in me. Remember that missive from my secret admirer?"

"That doesn't count." When she started to protest, he added, "I know you think it counts, but it doesn't. Unless a gentleman is willing to talk to you face to face, all the secret admirers in the world don't matter. You'll never get married if you never meet the person."

She closed her mouth. Maybe he was right, but that didn't mean her secret admirer's feelings for her were any less significant.

SECRET ADMIRER

"I suppose this secret admirer of yours could be Lord Swenson," her brother said as he dipped his quill into the ink. "If so, it's good he's finally stepping forward to make his intentions publicly known."

She decided not to respond. She really didn't think Lord Swenson was the gentleman who'd written her that wonderful note.

"There we are." Her brother finished writing the missive and put the quill back in its holder. He leaned back in his chair. "I was thinking of doing some shopping. Would you like to come with me? You can pick out a gown to wear for Lord Swenson's visit." He shrugged. "Or you can pick out a gown simply to have something new to wear."

She smiled at him. "You spoil me, Horatio."

"If you can't spoil your sister, who can you spoil?"

"I'm very lucky to have a brother like you. Let's go out. I don't need a gown, though." It would be nice to simply spend some time with him. The Season had been so busy that they hadn't had much time to relax and talk.

"All right. We won't go with the intention of you getting a gown. If, however, you find something that catches your fancy, feel free to get it." He stood up and retrieved the missive. "I'll have the butler send this out."

She didn't know why the thought of Edwin sending her brother's reply to Lord Swenson should make her feel uncertain, but it did. She released her breath and followed him out of the room.

———⁘———

IT WAS FUNNY HOW RACHEL had barely noticed Edwin while she ate dinner in the past. On this particular evening, she was acutely aware of him. How was it possible an innocent conversation earlier that day in the drawing room could change things so much?

"It's nice we're not hosting or attending a dinner party this evening," Horatio said.

Rachel glanced at Edwin as he poured wine into her brother's glass. His gaze met hers. She quickly turned her gaze back to her plate. The fact that he'd caught her looking at him shouldn't make her skin tingle. And yet, it did. She swallowed the roast pheasant and cut another piece from the tender meat.

"Do you want more wine?" Horatio asked her.

She noted that her glass was still pretty full and shook her head. Then, without meaning to, she watched as Edwin put the wine bottle back in its rightful place. She supposed he was quite attractive. He didn't wear the fancy clothes titled and wealthy gentlemen did. She wouldn't expect him to, not with him being a butler. But if he did wear something like those gentlemen wore, he would probably attract quite a few ladies who were seeking husbands. She forced her gaze back to her food and took another bite of the cooked pheasant. God willing, no one in this room knew what she was thinking. She'd die of embarrassment if anyone figured out her mind was on matters where it shouldn't be.

"I really am sorry last evening went so badly," her brother told her in a low voice. "I wish things were different for Carol. You do understand there is nothing I can do to stop the marriage, don't you?"

She smiled at her brother. "I know. The contract is binding. There's nothing anyone but her uncle can do about it." It was a shame her uncle wasn't like Horatio. But then, Horatio was a rare person. After a moment, she asked, "Isn't there a lady you fancy?"

Her brother shook his head. "I haven't met anyone I wish to marry yet. I do want to get married, but when I do, it'll be for love. I want someone who'll not only be the mother of my children but will be a friend, too."

Once more she wished he and Lydia would feel differently about each other. Lydia would be a wonderful wife, and he'd be a wonderful husband.

SECRET ADMIRER

"I'm still shocked suitors aren't trying to break down the door of this townhouse to see you," her brother continued as he poked his fork into the cooked carrot. "At the beginning of the Season, I fully expected you to have to agonize over which suitor you'd pick."

She had to resist the urge to glance in Edwin's direction. She didn't know why such talk should make her feel shy around him. She had shared personal conversations with her brother and friends many times when Edwin must have been in the room. And yet, suddenly, it was difficult for her to discuss these personal matters in front of him as if he wasn't there.

She cleared her throat. "I think it's because I don't know what to say around most people. If you've ever noticed, you're the one who does most of the talking at dinner parties."

"There's nothing wrong with being the person who listens." Shooting her a teasing grin, he added, "Who would let the rambler talk if there was no one willing to listen?"

She chuckled. "You don't ramble. Everything you say has a purpose."

"Maybe."

"It's true. You've put no one to sleep yet, so you're fine. You're a lot like Mother. She could talk to anyone. 'A stranger is a friend you haven't met yet,' is what she used to say. You seem to think the same way."

"Well, you can't get to know someone unless you talk to them."

"There you go. You just proved my point. You have a gift, Horatio. Sometimes I envy it."

"I don't know how I do it, Rachel. I open my mouth and words come out. You're shy, that's all. Once you get to know someone, you have no trouble talking to them. A gentleman just needs to spend enough time with you to make you comfortable."

"It's easy to talk to someone you're comfortable around." Once more, she had to resist the urge to glance Edwin's way. He had probably noticed that about her. Up until she had asked for his help in finding her secret admirer, she'd said very little to him. Now she had no trouble telling him what was on her mind. "It's also easy to talk to someone who cares about what you have to say." She'd said that specifically for Edwin's benefit, though she wasn't sure he would notice that. It wasn't like she could look directly at him so he'd know she had him in mind when she spoke those words.

Her brother nodded as he swallowed his food. "Yes, it does help when someone cares about what you have to say. One thing I noticed is that a lot of people in London are too wrapped up in how others perceive them. So much of this life is about impressing the right people. They'll say anything to get into the good graces of someone with influence. You don't know whether they are pretending to care or if they really do. You're fortunate to have your friends."

What a curious thing for her brother to say. "You have friends."

"Not like you do. The gentlemen I'm acquainted with aren't the same as your friends. The gentlemen are cordial, but we don't share the same depth of friendship that you, Lydia, and Carol do."

She would have suggested that it might be in the nature for ladies to share a deeper friendship, but for some reason, that didn't seem right. It shouldn't matter if one was a lady or a gentleman. A person's character was the important thing. Without meaning to, her gaze went to Edwin. He was collecting the dishes that were empty. Yes, he might be a butler, but he was more important than that to her.

"You might envy my ability to talk to others, but I envy you for your friendships," her brother said.

Her gaze went back to him, and she smiled. "That's not fair, Horatio. In addition to being my brother, you are also my friend."

He returned her smile. "I'm very grateful for that."

She returned his smile, and he began talking about the activities they would do for the next few days.

Chapter Thirteen

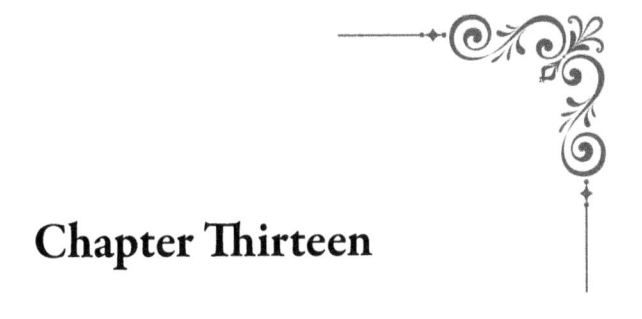

Edwin escorted Lord Swenson to the drawing room. Both Rachel and her brother were already waiting for the visitor. Edwin tried not to notice how lovely Rachel looked in her rose-colored gown. He liked her most in pink. That color brought out the color in her cheeks. As if she knew he was thinking about her in romantic terms, she made eye contact with him. Face warm, he hurried to look away.

"May I bring something to eat and drink?" Edwin asked her brother.

His Grace nodded. "Lord Swenson, what refreshments do you prefer?"

"I'm partial to cinnamon tea and scones," Lord Swenson replied.

His Grace turned to Edwin. "We'll have those."

Edwin had to resist the urge to take another look at Rachel before he left the room. There was no denying it. It was getting harder and harder to act like he wasn't in love with her. If he wasn't careful, someone would catch on, and if that happened, he would probably lose his job. There was no way he would be permitted to keep working here if anyone found out the truth.

But maybe that would be for the best. Did he really want to see her years in the future when she had a husband and children? He was having a difficult enough time with Lord Swenson here. The gnawing feeling in the pit of his stomach got worse. He supposed he could look for work elsewhere. After securing that job, he could quit this one. Then he wouldn't have to watch Rachel as she lived her happy life with someone who wasn't him.

When he reached the kitchen, he instructed Mr. Brown, the cook, to get tea ready then searched for the spices.

"What are you looking for?" Mrs. Brown asked as she came into the kitchen.

"The spices," Edwin replied. "Didn't we get a new supply of them from the market the other day?"

"Yes, we did. Mr. Brown and I moved things around the kitchen yesterday," she said. "The spices are over here now."

Edwin went to the other cupboard where they were.

She chuckled. "I've told you twice already that things have been moved around. Don't tell me you forgot."

Edwin ignored the teasing tone in her voice as he sorted through the spices. Lord Swenson wanted cinnamon.

Mrs. Brown studied him. "Will you remember where the spices are later today when you come in here for more tea?"

He found the cinnamon and turned his attention to her, noting the amused grin on her face. He cleared his throat. "There's been a lot on my mind. His Grace wants to host another dinner party in a week." And from the sound of it, His Grace was planning on inviting Lord Swenson if today's visit went well.

Mr. Brown arched an eyebrow. "You've served plenty of dinner parties. That wouldn't be pressing on your mind." A grin crossed his face. "I know what it is. You're thinking of a young woman."

Heat crept up his cheeks. The man could not possibly know that!

Mrs. Brown's eyes grew wide as she glanced at her husband. "You think so?"

"I don't think it. I know it." Mr. Brown took the kettle off of the stove and poured the hot water into the teapot. "I was once a young man. I remember how it was." He winked at her. "You were impossible to stop thinking about. I even accidently swapped salt with sugar for a meal once. Terribly embarrassing, that whole incident was. I'm just glad you married me so I could start concentrating on making meals the right way."

Mrs. Brown giggled and placed some cups on the tray. "I didn't know you had trouble cooking when I first came to this house to work."

"That's because I didn't tell you. Have no doubt about it. Mr. Morgan fancies someone." His gaze went to Edwin. "Mind telling us what maid it is and which household she works for?"

Edwin glanced from one to the other. Of course, they assumed it was a maid. No one would think he'd be foolish enough to fancy His Grace's sister. "I'd rather not say," he finally replied. "It's embarrassing enough you figured out I'm interested in someone."

"There's nothing to be embarrassed about," Mrs. Brown said. "Most people fall in love at some time in their lives. Tell me, does she return your feelings?"

Edwin brought the cinnamon to the tray then went to get the scones. "I'm certain she doesn't."

"Have you told her your feelings?" Mr. Brown asked.

"No," Edwin replied.

"Then how can you know she doesn't return them?" he pointed out.

Edwin thought over the best way to answer as he set the scones and folded cloth napkins on the tray. "The whole thing would never work."

"Maybe His Grace will agree to hire her so she can work here," Mrs. Brown said. "Or maybe he'll allow you to have your own little home so you two can live together. Not all employers expect their servants to go without marriage, and some don't mind it if a child is around so long as we make the child behave."

Edwin was only digging himself into a hole by answering these two. There would be no end to this conversation as long as he allowed it. He picked up the tray and cleared his throat. "I have no intention of acting on my feelings. I'm satisfied with things the way they are."

Though they looked disappointed, they didn't protest. Good. With that out of the way, he could go on with his job. He carried the tray out of the room.

When he returned to the drawing room, His Grace and Rachel were laughing at a story Lord Swenson was telling them.

"I can't say that all elephants are difficult to ride," Lord Swenson said. "But they don't like bees. The odd thing is that they don't even have to see the bees. The sound of a beehive is enough to send them into terror. My elephant flapped its ears and shook so hard that I almost fell off of it."

Edwin set the tray down. He tried not to notice that Lord Swenson was sitting a little too close to Rachel on the settee. He released his breath and poured tea into the cups.

"I've never been on an elephant," His Grace told Lord Swenson. "Are you sure they aren't dangerous?"

"They can be dangerous if you don't know how to treat them," Lord Swenson replied. "That's why you should be respectful and gentle with them. If you treat them well, they'll do the same to you."

"I think it's brave of you to ride one," Rachel commented. "I'd never go on one. They're so large."

Yes, Edwin supposed she would think Lord Swenson was brave for riding an elephant. Even Edwin wouldn't ride one if he was given the chance. It didn't seem like something a rational person would do. Why not just ride a horse?

"Elephants can be trained," Lord Swenson said. "It's best to train them when they're young. Then they learn not to fear humans early in life."

His Grace accepted the cup of tea Edwin handed out to him. "Perhaps I should take a trip to India sometime. It might be nice to check out another country. See the way other people live. See what customs they have."

SECRET ADMIRER

"Well, I'll tell you right now that you'll love the scenery." Lord Swenson accepted his cup then glanced at Rachel and smiled. "Though I will add that London has some lovely attractions, too."

It was a good thing people never noticed the servants because Edwin scowled at Lord Swenson. *Stop it, Edwin. He is a titled gentleman, and you're not. He has every right to compliment Rachel. And he's right. Rachel is a lovely sight. In fact, no lady can compare to her in beauty.*

Edwin forced himself to take on a neutral expression and held out a cup to Rachel. She offered him a smile and thanked him. Her fingers brushed his as she took the cup, sending pleasant tingles all through him. He resisted the urge to get on his knees and beg her to choose him even though he was nothing more than a butler. Mindful of His Grace, Edwin offered her a nod before turning to His Grace. When His Grace indicated he could leave, Edwin headed for the door.

"If you really want to see something wonderful, you might like the pyramids in Egypt," Lord Swenson said. "You hear stories of their majesty, but until you see them, you don't realize how awe-inspiring they are. I think your sister might enjoy the trip as well. Should things work out, I would be more than happy to introduce the both of you to a tour guide I know there."

Edwin rolled his eyes. It was just his luck that Lord Swenson was as charming as he seemed at the ball when Lord Swenson had made Rachel laugh. Edwin had no chance next to someone like that.

Listen to yourself, Edwin. You didn't have a chance with her to begin with. You are a butler. That is all. Noble ladies do not marry butlers. Remember your place.

Chapter Fourteen

Horatio cleared his throat to get Rachel's attention. Her cheeks warmed. She hadn't realized her brother had noticed that she'd been watching Edwin as he left the room. She forced her attention back to the conversation going on between Horatio and their guest.

"I have some drawings of the pyramids," Lord Swenson was saying. "If you wonder what they look like, the drawings will give you a good idea of what to expect if you ever go to Egypt. I drew them myself."

"You drew them?" Horatio asked.

"I did. I don't mean to brag, but the drawings are well done. I'm quite talented in the arts." Lord Swenson took a bite of his scone.

Horatio waited for Rachel to say something, but her mind was a complete blank. She offered him an apologetic shrug then sipped her tea.

Her brother thought for a moment then said, "Lady Rachel and I will have to discuss whether we can make a trip to Egypt. The estate is in good standing, but it's been a while since I worked through the accounts."

"With so much to do in London, I don't blame you," Lord Swenson said. "I let my steward handle the tedious task of managing the money. I'd rather visit with people and go to balls. People are a lot more interesting."

Rachel pretended not to notice the way Lord Swenson *accidentally* brushed her leg with his knee as he leaned to pour more tea into his cup. She wasn't very well acquainted with the way suitors were supposed to act, but it seemed to her that Lord Swenson was a little too forward. She wondered if her brother noticed it. She glanced at her brother, but his expression was neutral.

"Have you two had the pleasure of making Lord and Lady Cadwalader's acquaintance?" Lord Swenson asked as he leaned back on the settee.

Good. His knee was no longer touching her. Rachel relaxed. She didn't know if she was supposed to enjoy being *accidentally* touched. It seemed that Lord Swenson enjoyed *accidentally* touching her since this was the second time he'd done it during the visit. The first time had been when his elbow brushed hers while he sat down.

"No, I can't say we have," Horatio answered. "We don't have the influence that some people do. I think that's my fault. I'm more of a recluse. Lady Rachel's first Season has forced me to leave the townhouse."

Lord Swenson chuckled. "I was wondering why I just noticed her this Season." He glanced her way. "Someone so lovely is hard to miss."

Rachel was sure she was supposed to enjoy the compliment, but she didn't. Something about him was wrong. He was being charming. He was showing her interest. She should be thrilled, but for some reason, she wasn't.

He's not the one you want, Rachel. You want someone else.

The realization came to her so suddenly that her eyes grew wide. That was it. While she was flattered by his attention, she had no desire to marry him.

"Rachel," her brother spoke up, "why don't you tell Lord Swenson some of the things you like? We spent all of this time talking. It'd be nice to hear from you."

"Yes," Lord Swenson agreed, turning to her. "I want to know more about you."

Surprised to be the focus of the conversation, she glanced from one gentleman to the other. "I don't know what to say."

"Start by telling us what you like most," Horatio encouraged.

Oh. Well, that sounded easy enough, she supposed. Her gaze went to the doorway. Edwin hadn't returned. But then, he wouldn't until her brother summoned him. She straightened up and set the cup on the tray so she could clasp her hands in her lap. If she was going to participate in this conversation, she needed to focus.

"I like spending time with my friends," she offered.

"Don't we all?" Lord Swenson teased in a playful manner.

"Well, yes, I suppose we do. Otherwise, they wouldn't be friends," she said.

Lord Swenson laughed. "I like your wit, Lady Rachel. It's a refreshing change."

Her eyebrows furrowed. A refreshing change from what? What were ladies typically like?

He nudged her in the arm. "I'd like to hear something about your friends."

That was the third time he'd touched her in some way, but it had been the first time the touch had been meant to be seem intentional. And she didn't enjoy it any more than she'd enjoyed the others. There was only one gentleman she could think of whose touch she might enjoy, but she suspected her brother wouldn't be pleased if he found out.

She cleared her throat and forced her attention back to Lord Swenson and her brother. Thinking of Carol's guardian and how he was forcing her into a miserable marriage, she said, "I can trust my friends to care about what I have to say, and they don't try to force me to do something I don't want." Thinking of Lydia's ability to tolerate Lord Quinton, she continued, "They can accept me as I am." Thinking of her brother, she added, "They are thoughtful and considerate."

Lord Swenson smiled. "It sounds like you're surrounded by wonderful people."

"I am." Her gaze went to the doorway. She hadn't expected Edwin to be there. Her brother hadn't summoned him. But a part of her had hoped he might be. It was ironic how she hadn't noticed him for the longest time, and now she couldn't help but notice how often he was gone.

It had to be love. She couldn't recall a time when she'd longed for someone's company as much as she longed for Edwin's. It was possible Lord Swenson was her secret admirer, but since that missive came, she had gotten to know Edwin. This afternoon with Lord Swenson had shown her just how much she had come to care for Edwin without even realizing it.

Lord Swenson turned to Horatio. "I must commend you, Your Grace. You have done an excellent job in making your sister into a lady worth a gentleman's time and attention."

Her brother thanked him for the compliment, and the two continued to talk. She tried to pay attention, but she couldn't. Now that she realized her feelings for Edwin had gone beyond friendship, all she could do was ponder the best way to proceed from here.

RACHEL SAT AT THE VANITY in her bedchamber. She could have taken a walk, she supposed, but her brother would insist on joining her so she was chaperoned, and she didn't know if talking to him right now was the best option. She couldn't go to Edwin about her swirling emotions, either. Imagine him finding out she was in love with him! He would be shocked. He would remind her that she needed to be with a titled gentleman. She was the sister of a duke, after all. She couldn't marry a butler.

She glanced at her reflection in the mirror. "Why must there be so many rules on what a noble lady can and can't do?"

All the wealth around her implied she could do anything, and yet, she was trapped. Just how was she supposed to fall in love with someone else when Edwin was the only gentleman she could think about?

SECRET ADMIRER

A knock came at her door. Glad for the distraction, she jumped out of the chair and went to open it.

The maid said, "Miss Lydia Hamilton is here. Are you up to receiving visitors?"

Rachel nodded. "I'll see her. Don't bother telling her. I'll go down right now."

Rachel hurried down the stairs, only thinking too late that it would be unseemly for her to be running. Thankfully, Edwin wasn't anywhere in sight, so she was spared any embarrassment.

Lydia ran over to her as soon as she entered the drawing room. "I'm glad you're here. I wasn't sure if you'd be out with Lord Swenson. I only remembered that you were supposed to see him today after I came here."

"He was already here. Your timing is fine." Rachel turned to the doorway. Usually, Edwin would come into the room to offer them something to eat or drink, but instead of Edwin, one of the maids came in. Without thinking, she blurted out, "Where is the butler?"

"He's out buying wine," the maid replied. "Can I get anything for you and Miss Hamilton?"

Rachel glanced her friend's way.

Lydia shook her head. "I'm too nervous to eat or drink anything."

"We won't be having anything at the moment, thank you," Rachel told the maid. She waited until the maid left the room then shut the door. "What is it, Lydia?"

Lydia bit her lower lip then blurted out, "I need to know where Lord Quinton lives."

"Why?"

"Because I'm going to marry him."

Rachel's eyes grew so wide she thought they were going to pop out of her head. "I didn't realize he proposed. Why didn't you tell me he was courting you?"

Lydia's face grew pink, and she offered Rachel a tentative smile. "Well, that's just it. He hasn't proposed. In fact, I've only seen him once since your brother's dinner party. Unfortunately, he was too far away for me to call out to him before he went into White's. But I don't think you need to know someone for a long time to figure out you're meant to be together. Marriages happen all the time where the lady and gentleman hardly know each other."

"I don't think you need to know someone for long to marry them, either, but in this case, you're assuming Lord Quinton wants to marry you."

"We belong together. I know it as much as I know my own soul. The more I find out about him, the more I'm in love with him."

"If you haven't talked to him since my brother's dinner party, how can you know more about him?"

"Felix asked some gentlemen he knows about him."

Rachel frowned. "Felix didn't actually talk to him?"

"No. Whenever Lord Quinton sees Felix heading in his direction, he runs off in another direction."

"Does Lord Quinton know Felix is your brother?"

"No. Felix has never met him before. I tried to talk my other brother into talking to Lord Quinton, but Oscar hasn't been able to find him any time he's been out. That's why we need to know where Lord Quinton lives. I was thinking that since your brother invited Lord Quinton to the dinner party, he must know Lord Quinton's address."

"Yes, he does, but are you sure you want to be with Lord Quinton? He's stranger than other gentlemen."

"I don't mind someone who is superstitious," Lydia assured her. "There are greater flaws a gentleman can have. Besides, he was incredibly sweet at the dinner party." Before Rachel could speak, she hurried to add, "I don't have any suitors, and the estate is suffering. My brothers can't find any fathers who are willing to let their daughters marry a pauper. Our only hope is for me to find a wealthy gentleman. I'd like to marry someone I'm interested in who, I believe, is interested in me."

"How can you believe Lord Quinton is interested in you if he hasn't made an attempt to find you?"

"Does he know where I live?"

"Wouldn't Lord Quinton ask Horatio where you live if he wanted to talk to you?" Rachel pointed out.

"I'm not sure he would come here since Horatio made it clear he doesn't like him."

"If Lord Quinton came here, Horatio would talk to him. Horatio wouldn't be rude to him."

"Does Lord Quinton know that? I caught the way Lord Wright and Horatio talked about Lord Quinton under their breaths during the dinner party. I'm sure Lord Quinton picked up on it, too."

Yes, Rachel had noticed that neither gentleman cared all that much for Lord Quinton. If she was Lord Quinton, she wouldn't want to come by to pay Horatio a visit, either. "All right. I'll ask my brother where Lord Quinton lives."

"Thank you!"

Rachel began to leave the room but then thought over her own dilemma and turned back to her friend. "Lydia, do you really think it's important to marry Lord Quinton of all people?"

"After watching everything Carol is going through, I have no doubt about it. You have to be with someone you can share a love match with. What good is marriage if it's to the wrong person?"

Her friend was right. Carol might have all the money she'd ever want, but she was going to be miserable. The money just wasn't worth it. Quite frankly, marrying a titled gentleman wasn't worth it, either. Marriage was for a lifetime, and a lifetime was a long time to spend with the wrong person. That meant Rachel would be much better off with a butler than with someone else.

"I'll talk to Horatio," Rachel told her friend then left the drawing room.

She ended up finding him in the library, and though he had a book open on his lap, he was staring out the window.

He turned his gaze in her direction as she approached him. He closed the book, set it on the small table next to him, and rose to his feet. "Lord Swenson asked me if he could be your suitor after you went to your bedchamber."

She had worried he might do that.

"As your brother," he began, "I feel it necessary to suggest that you look elsewhere for a husband."

She hadn't expected this. "You do?"

"I know he's charming and good looking, but he's way too forward. It took all of my willpower not to smack him every time he touched you. If he's that open while I'm around, I can only imagine what he does when there's no chaperone in the room."

Before he went on, she put her hand on his arm. "I don't want to marry him, Horatio. You can tell him he can't be my suitor."

He didn't hide his relief. "I worried you would be upset."

"No, I'm not upset. The truth is, I wasn't all that pleased with how often he touched me, either. I thought you two got along so well that you'd push for the match."

"I had to be a gracious host. Though, I will tell you it wasn't easy." He put his hand over his stomach and released his breath. "So, you didn't come in here to ask me what Lord Swenson and I were talking about after you left the drawing room?"

"No, I came here because Lydia wants to know where Lord Quinton lives."

He blinked in surprise. "Why on earth would she want to know that?"

"She's in love with him."

He blinked again. "You're jesting."

"I'm sorry to say I am not," she replied with a giggle. "Lydia has decided that Lord Quinton is the gentleman she'll marry."

"After his behavior at the dinner party, how is this possible? I thought Lydia had more sense than that."

"Well, she might have had some sense if you ever offered her your hand in marriage, but since you didn't, she had to look elsewhere."

"And Lord Quinton is the best she could come up with?"

She shrugged. What could she say? Lydia had her mind made up. Lord Quinton was the only gentleman she was interested in marrying. "If she'll be happy with him, does it matter what we think of him?"

"No. I suppose there are worse sins a man can commit than trading partners at a dinner party and then complaining about the food. He's annoying, but he's not dangerous." He went to the desk and wrote the address down. "I hope she'll be happy with him."

"Even if he is peculiar, he is better than the Duke of Augustine." Now there was a marriage that was going to be terrible. "Thank you for not forcing me to marry someone like that."

He gave her the paper, and she ran her fingers along the edge of it. "What would you have thought if Lydia wanted to marry a servant?"

His eyebrows furrowed. "I thought she needed to marry someone with money."

"Let's say she didn't need money. Let's say her family had good financial standing. Do you think love is more important than money?"

"I think when it comes to marriage, Lydia needs to think with her head and her heart. She'd be better off with a titled gentleman or one with money. There are enough of those gentlemen to choose from, especially since her brothers aren't forcing her to marry someone in particular."

Rachel thought about protesting that the servant might be so wonderful that all of the acceptable gentlemen in London failed in comparison to him, but she decided against it in case her brother figured out she wasn't really talking about Lydia.

Besides, she didn't even know if Edwin loved her. While she was certain he didn't just think of her as his employer's sister, he might only think of her as a friend. If that was the case, then all of this fretting was for nothing. Thanking Horatio for the address, she left the room so she could give it to Lydia.

Chapter Fifteen

Edwin held off on returning to the townhouse for as long as he could, but, unfortunately, the errands on his list didn't take up that much time. After he finished organizing the wine in the cellar, he trudged to his quarters. He intentionally avoided the other servants. He already knew Lord Swenson wanted to be Rachel's suitor. Someone would have to be a simpleton not to notice Lord Swenson's attraction to her, and it seemed as if Rachel was attracted to him, too.

But you knew the day would come when she found someone to marry. You're a butler. You could never be with her.

He removed the employment ads from his pocket and unfolded the paper. He had picked the ads up while he was out collecting things for the household. He really needed to find a job in another household. Given his age, it might require him to start at a lower level, but he couldn't stay here and watch Rachel come over with her husband and children when she wanted to see her brother.

He read through a couple of ads when the bell rang. That bell came from the drawing room. He let out a heavy sigh. The last thing he felt like doing was listening to Rachel or her brother talk about how wonderful Lord Swenson was. But, he had a job to do. Soon enough, he would no longer be working here, so the sting would only last for a little while.

He folded the paper then slipped it into the top drawer of his desk. When he reached the drawing room, he was surprised to see that

Rachel was waiting for him in the doorway. He peered into the room and saw that no one else was there.

"Do you want some tea or crumpets?" he asked.

"Oh, Edwin, you don't need to be so formal with me." Rachel waved him into the room.

He hesitated to go in there. She wasn't going to tell him all about her visit with Lord Swenson, was she? Because if that was her plan, he simply didn't have the stomach for it. He was doing good to perform his duties without giving away his despair.

She glanced down the hall, and seeing it empty, she took him by the arm and led him into the room. He was too startled to stop her. Every time she touched him, that pleasant warmth swept all through him, and he was enjoying that sensation way too much.

She shut the door. "There. Now no one can hear us."

Breaking out of his trance, he hurried to open it. "We can't allow this kind of thing to happen, my lady," he whispered. "The others will assume we're having an inappropriate conversation." Or they would assume something worse was going on.

But, instead of listening to reason, she shut the door. "I need to talk to you in private, and I don't want anyone to hear us."

"Don't you realize how bad that looks?"

"I don't care what others think."

"You should. I'm the butler. I have no business being in here with you, especially with the door closed."

She jumped in front of him before he could open the door again. "I have something important I wish to discuss with you. There is no other place where we can talk, and I can't have my brother here."

"Why not?"

"He wouldn't approve of it."

"There's a good reason for that. You're a noble lady, and I'm a butler. Even if I wasn't a butler, it would look bad. Lord Swenson was just here.

SECRET ADMIRER

What would he think if he knew we were in here without your brother to make sure nothing inappropriate was going on?"

"Lord Swenson is of no concern."

He wasn't? Edwin stared at her in shock. "Are you saying that Lord Swenson isn't your suitor?"

"No, he's not."

Well, this was a turn of events Edwin didn't expect. He thought for sure that Lord Swenson was interested in her. He'd been complimenting her and touching her enough. He had even made it sound like he was going to marry her and take her on all sorts of exotic trips.

"What's wrong with him?" Edwin asked, unable to hide his shock. "Doesn't he realize that no other lady can match you in beauty or in kindness?"

She gasped. "It's you. You're my secret admirer."

His face grew hot. There was no way she could know that. He'd been careful not to give his feelings away. In a panic, he lied, "No, I'm not."

"It has to be you. I've read that missive many times. I know the words by heart. *Lady Rachel Abbot, there is no lady more lovely than you. No one can match you in beauty or in kindness.* You just said, 'no other lady can match you in beauty or in kindness.' It can't be a coincidence that you just worded things that way."

He struggled to come up with some excuse, no matter how ridiculous, to convince her she was wrong, but his mind went blank. He hadn't been prepared for this. He hadn't realized she was going to take the words he'd written and memorize them.

She smiled. "This is wonderful."

"How can it be wonderful? We can't be together."

"Why not?"

Really? He had to explain it to her? "I'm a servant."

"You also wrote, *At night, I dream of you and wish for a future where we might be together. There will never be anyone for me but you.* Were you lying when you wrote that?"

"No, of course not. I wouldn't write it if I didn't mean it. That would have been cruel."

"Then that means you love me."

Oh dear. How was he to know that his words would come back to haunt him?

"It's all right, Edwin, because I love you, too," she said.

"You do? But how... When?"

She shrugged. "I don't know when it happened. I didn't even realize it until Lord Swenson was here. Edwin, I want to be with you."

"But Lord Swenson can give you this kind of life." He gestured to the room around them. "And I can't."

"My friend is about to spend the rest of her life with a wealthy gentleman who resents having to marry her. Do you think she's going to be happy even though she'll have a lot of money?"

He winced. He recalled her telling him about her friend. "No, she probably won't."

"What good is money if you're miserable? I don't want to be miserable, Edwin. Some things are more important than money. Love is one of them. I love you, and you love me. We could marry someone that we don't love, but what good will that do us or them? Wouldn't it be better if we married each other? Then we can be with the one we really want, and we can let those people find someone who will love them as they should be loved."

He studied her, just to make sure he was understanding what she was saying. He'd wanted so much for her to tell him these things that, for a moment, he worried this was a trick of his imagination. But she continued to smile at him in a way that made him feel as if he could float right on up to the clouds. She was offering him the opportunity to spend a lifetime with her. He didn't have to stay in the shadows and watch as she married someone else and had someone else's children. He could get the chance to be her husband, and she'd have his children.

The last of his resolve faded. He cupped the side of her face with his hand and stroked her cheek with his thumb. She was still smiling at him. He took that as an invitation to kiss her, so he did. As soon as their lips touched, a surge of pleasure coursed through his body. He had often dreamt of how kissing her might be, and this was far better than anything he could imagine.

He ended the kiss. "Are you sure you want to do this?" he whispered.

"I've never been more sure of anything," she replied.

Well, that settled it. If he turned his back on this moment, he would regret it for the rest of his life. Perhaps it was foolish for them to marry, but he would rather die than live without her. Why should he say no when she wanted to be with him, too?

"I love you, Rachel," he said. "I might not have a lot of money, but I have enough to rent a small place, and I learned a lot in my time as a butler of this house. I'll work hard to provide for you and our children, and I promise I'll love you with everything I have until the day I die." Then he sealed the promise with a kiss.

Chapter Sixteen

The next couple of days passed by in a blur. To avoid being stopped from eloping, Rachel and Edwin had chosen to leave in the middle of the night. Edwin had rented the carriage and the driver to take them to Gretna Green.

Rachel did leave a note for her brother so he wouldn't worry about her. *I realize he's a butler,* she had written, *but I know he's going to be good to me. He'll love me the way you hoped one of the titled gentlemen would love me. Please don't worry about us. Edwin has some money set aside that we will use. We're going to Gretna Green. I will write more when we return to London.*

She knew the note had been brief, but she couldn't think of what else to write. She'd much rather have a longer discussion with her brother in person. She realized there was a small possibility he might annul the marriage. She wasn't twenty-one, and her brother was her guardian. She could only hope that by the time she and Edwin returned to London that her brother would have sufficient time to accept the marriage.

On the day they arrived in Gretna Green, Rachel was relieved. Being alone with Edwin in the carriage provided them a lot of time to kiss each other, and though they slept in separate rooms during the night, she was having trouble not doing more than she should. She had no idea that the desire to be touched and kissed could be so powerful when she wanted to be with someone. If it had been Edwin rather than Lord

Swenson who'd given her those little touches on the settee, she would have enjoyed them immensely.

"Let's get married before we go to the inn," Rachel said as she peered out the window.

It was early in the afternoon. Surely, there was plenty of time to get a room for the night.

"I'm just as eager as you are to get married," Edwin replied, "but I don't know if you can just walk into a blacksmith's shop and have the ceremony done right away. The priest might be busy."

Her shoulders slumped in disappointment before she turned back to face him. "I hadn't thought of that." She was so used to everyone around her being ready to do whatever she wanted at a moment's notice. She was going to have to get used to doing things differently.

"Why don't we get a room now, and then I'll ask the priest when he'll be ready to marry us."

She was about to ask him what would happen if the priest wasn't going to be able to marry them until tomorrow, but he kissed her, and she forgot the question that lingered on her mind. It was like this every time he kissed her. The rest of the world slipped away. It was the most peculiar sensation, but it was also incredibly wonderful. It was proof that she was meant to be with him.

Edwin retrieved their valises from the floor. "It's still early in the day. I have no doubt we'll be married by evening. I'm so certain of it that I'm only going to pay for one room."

The thought of spending the night in bed with him made her skin warm with a mixture of anticipation and shyness. When they were caught up in kissing, it was easy to forget that the unknown made her a bit nervous. But he loved her. He had loved her for a lot longer than she'd imagined. During the trip, he had told her about the moment he had fallen in love with her. She wouldn't have guessed he'd felt that way for such a long time. He'd never given her any clues she could detect. It was to her good fortune that he'd written her the missive. Otherwise, she would have missed on having a love match.

Edwin opened the door and stepped out of the carriage. He turned to Rachel, and since he was holding a valise in each hand, she took his arm so she could join him.

"I must say, it's nice to see two people in love," the driver said as he approached them. "I've done quite a few trips to Gretna Green in my time, and the couples who marry here are often much happier than those who marry in London. I suppose in London most people marry because they have to. It's always better when you can marry because you want to."

Edwin glanced at her and smiled. "There's no one else I'd rather have."

Returning his smile, she voiced her agreement.

"This inn is a favorite among the people I take to Gretna Green." The driver motioned to the building in front of them. "I'm acquainted with the innkeeper. He's a good man. Treats his guests and staff right. You'll enjoy staying here." He gestured across the street to a building down to the left. "You'll find the priest in the blacksmith's shop down there. You tell him Hank took you here, and he'll go easy on you with the payment."

As the driver went to take care of the horses, Edwin led her into the inn. "I can see why he gets plenty of business," Edwin told her in a low voice. "He has a good attitude. I aspire to be like that."

"You don't need to aspire to be that way. You already are like that." She squeezed his arm. "I'm not worried about our future. I know you'll be able to take care of me."

"I once heard that a good lady can do wonders for a gentleman. Now I know how true that is." He opened the door and gestured for her to go in first. "I'm going to do everything in my power to be deserving of you."

She used to think nothing could be better than reading that missive he'd written anonymously, but the words he spoke were even better. At his heart, he was far more romantic than she could have ever dreamed. If he had talked to her like this when they were in London, she might have figured out he was her secret admirer much sooner. Well, she supposed that didn't matter now. What mattered was that she had figured it out before she ended up with the wrong person. She didn't have to settle for second best. She was going to have the best.

WHEN EDWIN WOKE UP the next morning, his first thought was that everything had been a dream. One very long and wonderful dream. There was no way Rachel had found out he was her secret admirer then asked him to go all the way to Gretna Green to marry her.

He was certain that he would open his eyes and find himself in his room in the Duke of Creighton's townhouse. He would be on a small, but comfortable, bed. The desk, where he kept the wine ledger, would be to his right. The keys to the china cabinet and wine cellar would be on the hook by the door. His first order of business would be to wash up and get dressed. Then he would check on the drawing room and the library to make sure they were ready for His Grace and Rachel. After that, life would go on as normal.

He let out a sigh of disappointment. It was too bad that dreams passed by so fast. He would like to stay in bed and linger in the dream-world forever.

The mattress under him moved. Then someone incredibly soft and curvy snuggled up to him and kissed his cheek. He'd had vivid dreams before, but nothing was ever this detailed.

He opened his eyes and was surprised to see that Rachel was looking down at him. Her dark hair was ruffled and hanging in dark waves down her shoulders, and her face was flushed from all the activity they had shared in bed the previous evening.

He blinked the sleep from his eyes. "Did we really get married?"

She kissed him. "Don't tell me that yesterday was so boring that you forgot about our wedding."

He grinned and wrapped his arms around her. "I thought it was all a dream. It seemed too good to be true."

"Well, it's not. After we got to Gretna Green, we got a room at this inn and then married. You remember the priest, don't you?"

"A balding round fellow who had a parrot that repeated the last word of every sentence he said?"

She chuckled. "Yes, that's the one. He used to be a pirate before he gave his life to the Lord. The only thing he kept from his past was that bird."

Yes, Edwin remembered the story the priest had told them about that parrot. "Did he really name the thing Treasure?"

"He did. He said it was the best thing he found in all his travels." She gave him another kiss then offered him a sly grin. "Do you remember what we did after the wedding?"

He supposed he could be good and give her the answer she was expecting, but another part of him opted for some mischief. "I don't remember anything after the wedding. You're going to have to spur my memory."

Amused, she traced his jaw with her finger. "We had something to eat. It was good stew."

"Ah, stew. Yes, now I'm remembering eating." He let his hand slide down to her hip. "That was good stew."

"It was so good you couldn't stop eating it. The innkeeper worried there wouldn't be enough left for anyone else after you had your tenth bowl."

His eyes grew wide. "A tenth bowl?"

Her eyebrows rose innocently. "I had to ask some people to help me tear you from the table because you weren't ready to be alone with me in this room. All you wanted to do was keep on eating. I was beginning to worry you didn't want to be alone with me," she continued with a cute pout. "I had no idea that I was going to have to compete with a bowl of stew for your affections."

With a mock gasp, he got up on his side then rolled her onto her back. "How dare you accuse me of not being attentive to your every need? I'll have you know I take my role as a husband seriously."

She laughed and put her arms around his shoulders. "You were most attentive. I enjoyed all of last night."

"That's better." He smiled then gave her a lingering kiss.

One might think his enthusiasm for exploring her would have subsided already, given how much he'd been able to do last night, but his erection urged him to do more with her before leaving the bed. She didn't seem to mind since she let out a moan and pulled him closer to her.

Encouraged, he left a trail of kisses from her neck and worked his way down to her breasts. He recalled how excited he'd been to see her cleavage while they'd been in London. At the time, he hadn't imagined he would one day get to touch her breasts. Sure, he had wanted to. But he never thought he'd get the opportunity to do it. It turned out to be better than he had expected. And she certainly seemed to enjoy being fondled since she murmured his name and wove her fingers through his hair.

After some time, he decided to explore more of her. He had touched the area between her legs last night. He was familiar with the wet warmth that awaited him. But the shadows in the room had made it difficult to see this part of her. This morning, there was plenty of light for him to see all of her. He took a moment to scan her entire body. Every bit of her was even more beautiful than he dreamed possible.

He brought his mouth back to hers as he traced the folds of her flesh. She spread her legs further apart and lifted her hips so he could slide a couple of fingers into her. He moaned along with her. She was so wet. He had been far too excited last night to stroke her for long, but this morning, he had enough control over his erection that he explored this part of her in earnest.

He suspected she was enjoying what he was doing since her moans grew louder, but it wasn't until she pressed the palm of his hand against her sensitive nub and began rocking her hips that he realized this was bringing her significant pleasure. She had expressed her enthusiasm while making love to him last night, but this was different. This was a heightened state of pleasure she was experiencing. Eager to find out where this was going, he continued his ministrations. He didn't know what was more erotic: her bouncing breasts or the enraptured expression on her face that told him she wanted nothing more than to keep doing this with him. Both were exquisite. Both made him so hard that his body was urging him to enter her. But he held off. He wanted her to reach her peak. And when she did, the wait was worth it. He felt immense satisfaction in knowing he had given her this experience. He hadn't done it last night. Last night, he had received the intense pleasure. Now, it was only right she get what was due to her.

When she relaxed, he rose up and got between her legs. She wrapped her legs around his waist and pulled him into her. He closed his eyes and groaned. It felt just as good as it had last night. He might have had the patience to go slower if he hadn't been so aroused from watching her climax. He recalled being able to spend considerable time thrusting into her last night after they'd had their first time, but thinking of how he was able to bring her to completion was his undoing. He managed to get several thrusts in before he couldn't hold off anymore. He grew taut and filled her with his seed. He held onto her and rode out the waves of pleasure as they crashed into him.

When he descended back to Earth, he continued holding her for a long time. A part of him still couldn't believe this was real. But real or not, he was going to enjoy every moment of it.

Chapter Seventeen

Rachel thought she wasn't going to have to deal with her brother until she returned to London, but while she and Edwin were taking a walk through the market, she saw Horatio's carriage. She twisted the edge of her coat sleeve. She wasn't ready for the confrontation, but since her brother was here, she didn't see how she could delay it.

She turned to Edwin who was peering into the window of a shop where ledgers were sold. "Edwin, my brother's here."

He turned from the window and followed her gaze. "Do you think he plans to annul the marriage?"

Noting the worried tone in his voice, she admitted, "I don't think him coming here is a good sign. I had hoped that he would calm down during my absence and realize you and I make a good match." She put her hand in his. "Let me talk to him. Maybe I can reason with him."

He shifted from one foot to the other and let out an uneasy sigh. "Rachel, I know he has the right to separate us, but if he wants to annul this marriage, will you go to another country with me? I had a hard enough time pining for you while I was your butler. Now that we've been together romantically, there will be nothing for me if you're not in my life."

She couldn't imagine life without him, either. She squeezed his hand. "I won't let him separate us. He can't force me to go with him with all these people around. If I find out he wants to annul this marriage, I'll come right back to you, and we'll figure out what to do."

After a moment, he nodded. "All right. I'll wait for you in that gazebo over there." He gestured to the wood gazebo decorated in ribbons that was a few shops down from where they were standing.

She squeezed his hand again. "Regardless of what happens, I'll be there soon."

She didn't know if it was the wind or trepidation, but a chill swept through her. She pulled the coat more closely around herself and proceeded toward the carriage. It wasn't far from the stationary shop, but the time it took to reach it seemed to span an eternity. She glanced back and saw that Edwin was at the gazebo. He wasn't sitting on the bench. He just stood there with a worried frown on his face. She offered him a hopeful smile then turned her attention back to the carriage. When she reached it, she was surprised to find that her brother wasn't in it.

"Good afternoon, Lady Rachel," the coachman greeted.

She nodded a greeting in return. "Where is His Grace?"

"He's going around town looking for you. Would you like me to tell him you're waiting for him?"

She shook her head. "I'll wait for him here."

They fell into silence, and her gaze went back to Edwin. He still wasn't sitting. He had moved to the arched opening as if he was contemplating the idea of going to her. She could only imagine what the coachman was thinking. Edwin had been the butler. She took a deep breath and released it. Well, this was bound to be awkward regardless of whether the coachman was here or not.

When her brother came out of an inn further down the road, she strengthened her resolve and headed for him. He picked up his pace as soon as he noticed her.

"Thank goodness I found you," Horatio called out. He waited until he reached her before adding, "Am I too late for the wedding?"

"Yes, you are too late." Despite her shaky voice, she continued, "We married yesterday. Edwin is at the gazebo. I asked him to wait there while I talk to you. Horatio, I implore you to reconsider annulling our marriage."

"Annulling your marriage?"

She fiddled with the edge of her coat sleeve. "I know how much you wanted me to marry a gentleman with a title or money, but sometimes you can't help who you fall in love with. I love Edwin. If I didn't marry him, I was going to spend the rest of my life regretting it. Edwin might not have much, but his feelings for me are true. Maybe you have to be a lady to understand how important love is, but I'd rather be happy than live in a big house with a lot of things and servants at my command."

He put his hand on her arm. "Rachel, slow down. Take a deep breath."

She forced herself to do as he urged. Her heart was hammering so hard in her chest that she thought it might burst. He was right. She needed to calm down. It was hard to think clearly, let alone come up with a convincing argument. She didn't want to have to choose between Edwin and her brother, but if she had to, then she'd have to go with Edwin.

"I didn't come here to annul the marriage," Horatio gently told her.

She blinked in surprise. "You didn't?"

"No. I came to witness the wedding."

She blinked again. "You did?"

"You're my sister. I didn't want to miss the most important day of your life." He paused. "Though, I did since you just said you already married him. I thought I was rushing the poor coachman, but you two were faster."

All she could do was could was stare at him. Was she understanding him right? He really hadn't come to end the marriage?

He offered her a smile. "Rachel, I want you to be happy. I didn't realize when you were talking about noble ladies marrying servants that you were talking about you and Edwin. I thought you were talking about Lydia." He glanced around the people around them before he gestured for her to go with him to a more secluded spot.

She gave another glance at Edwin, and since he would still be able to see them, she followed her brother to a place where they could speak more freely.

"You're my sister," Horatio began. "Ever since we were children, you've been my closest friend. Sometimes you're the only person I can confide in. I understand why you were afraid to tell me how you felt about Edwin, but it hurt when I realized you were afraid to come to me about this. Did your friends know that you were going to come here to marry him?"

"No. I didn't tell anyone about it. I'm sorry, Horatio. I didn't mean to make you feel left out. I just didn't want you to stop me."

He relaxed. "I don't want us to stop being close."

"Horatio, we will always be good friends. That won't change. And who knows? Maybe you and Edwin can be friends. He's a wonderful person. He's much better than Lord Swenson or any other gentlemen I met this Season."

"A lot of gentlemen are better than Lord Swenson. It turns out he likes to jump from one bed to another." He grimaced. "If I'd known that beforehand, I never would have agreed to have him over for a visit."

"Well, you don't have anything to worry about. Edwin is nothing like him. I want you to talk to him. Get to know him the way I do. When you do, you'll understand why I married him."

His gaze went to Edwin then back to her. "All right. But I have something else to tell you first."

Sensing that this was going to be serious, she asked, "What is it?"

"The Duke of Augustine hung himself."

She gasped. "Did he do it to get out of the marriage to Carol?"

"That's what his note said."

How terrible. Granted, Carol had been dreading the marriage, but Rachel was certain Carol hadn't expected this turn of events. "What's going to happen to her?"

"I don't know. I only found out the news when a messenger sent this missive." He retrieved an envelope from his pocket and handed it to her. "This is from Carol. I thought it had something to do with your elopement, so I read it."

She took it from him and opened it. While Carol seemed relieved she didn't have to marry the Duke of Augustine, she also worried what her guardian was going to do.

"I took the liberty of writing to Lord Wright to let him know she is available before I left London," her brother continued. "I don't know if Lord Wright will be interested in marrying her, but I know he needs a mother for his child."

Maybe that would work. Lord Wright seemed like a much more pleasant person than the Duke of Augustine had been. Rachel didn't want anything bad to happen to anyone, but was it wrong that a part of her was glad her friend didn't have to marry him?

"Now that we have that unpleasantness aside, I would like to talk to Edwin," her brother suggested.

She folded the missive and slipped it into her coat pocket. They crossed the busy street, and she led her brother to the gazebo where Edwin was still waiting for her. It seemed to her that Edwin had spent a considerable amount of time waiting for her. And it was hard not to want to run up to him and thank him for writing that missive. Because of him, she didn't have to worry about her future like Carol or Lydia did. She knew she was going to be loved for the rest of her life.

With a smile, she slipped her arm around Edwin's. "Horatio came to congratulate us on our marriage."

Edwin's surprised gaze went to her brother.

"It's true," Horatio said. "I admit I was hesitant to agree to this arrangement when I first read the note Rachel left me, but you've always been steadfast at your job. You pay attention to detail. You take great care with your tasks. You never speak out of turn. You're polite, even when some guests are unreasonable. All in all, I think you'll make my sister a good husband."

"So you approve of the marriage?" Edwin asked, still not sounding sure of what he was hearing.

Horatio laughed. "Yes, I do. Rachel worried I was going to annul the marriage, but I assure you both that I won't. This is an untraditional arrangement. There's bound to be some who won't approve. But then, you can't please everyone all the time. Why not follow your heart and let those people worry about themselves?"

Edwin relaxed. "Thank you, Your Grace."

"We're family now. You can address me as Horatio. I'm going to give you my sister's dowry. After we return to London, I want you to find a good townhouse and suitable furniture so my sister will be able to live in the manner she's accustomed to. I never want her to lack for anything."

"I'll give her everything she needs," Edwin promised.

"I didn't think it was going to be this hard when it came time to hand my sister off to someone else," Horatio admitted, his voice growing soft. "But at least I know she's going to be under the care of someone who'll love her."

"You're going to make me cry if you keep this up," Rachel warned her brother and quickly wiped a tear from her eye.

"A brother has the right to get sentimental, doesn't he?" Horatio grinned then said, "I think that about settles everything I have to say. Now, I want you to tell me all about the courtship you had right under my nose. I've been dying to hear how this unlikely arrangement occurred."

Rachel decided it might be best if she started the story, so, after they sat down, she said, "Well, it all started when I received a note from my secret admirer."

SECRET ADMIRER

And for the next hour, she and Edwin filled him in on the details.

Don't Miss these Other Books in the Marriage by Obligation Series:

Midnight Wedding (Book 2)

Miss Lydia Hamilton enlists the help of her two brothers to kidnap Lord Quinton so she can marry him. While Lord Quinton isn't as opposed to the union as she fears, he does worry that being stranded out in the country where suspicious things are going on is the worst place for a honeymoon.

This is a steamy historical romantic comedy with a superstitious hero, a heroine who needs money, and an estate with a classic gothic feel to it. The hero and heroine are both virgins.

The Earl's Jilted Bride (Book 3)

The wallflower who was never loved...

Lady Carol was supposed to marry the Duke of Augustine. Then, shortly before the wedding, the duke committed suicide, citing her for the reason he couldn't go on living anymore. While there was no love lost between them, her situation is not any better when her guardian threatens to send her off to a convent unless she finds someone else to marry. Marriage to a gentleman she barely knows is a risky venture, but with nothing to lose, she accepts Lord Wright's hasty proposal. But she doesn't dare hope for a love match, until she gets to know him.

The widower who needs a mother for his young child...

Grant Carnel, Lord Wright, did everything he could to make everyone think he had a wonderful first marriage. He did it to protect the young child that isn't really his. He is determined that no one will learn the truth. His daughter's life will be free from scandal. With his first wife gone, he is free to marry again. But marriage would mean opening up old wounds that he thought he left behind. Especially when a gentleman comes around showing more interest in Carol than he has the right to have.

Two insecure people who were never loved are about to find out if love matches are possible in a place like London.

This is a steamy historical romance with a virgin heroine.

Worth the Risk (Book 4)

He's been a recluse his entire life...

All of his life, Mr. Reuben St. George has been sickly. His older brother has done everything he could to keep him safe and healthy, so for all of Reuben's life, he's been forced to stay in the country. When he's allowed to go to London to attend a Season, he finds the perfect lady to marry: Miss Amelia Carnel.

Unfortunately, London is a big place with a lot of people, and all it does is make him sick. As a result, he's unable to attend quite a few social activities. The most frustrating part is that Amelia has other suitors. Healthy suitors who can give her a normal life. As much as he hates to admit it, his brother is right. He needs to return to the country and let Amelia stay in London so she can marry someone who can give her the kind of life she deserves.

He never bothered to ask Amelia what she wants, and she's going to make certain he finds out.

*This is a steamy historical romance with a virgin hero and a virgin heroine.

Anyone But the Marquess (Book 5)

Felix Hamilton, the Marquess of Roland, really messed things up when, in a drunken stupor, he spread lies about her not being a virgin. Now there is little talk of nothing else. To make things right, Felix goes to Elizabeth's guardian to arrange a marriage with her. But Elizabeth is

SECRET ADMIRER

not one who can so easily forgive the one gentleman who ruined not only her reputation, but her life as well.

*This is a steamy historical romance with a virgin hero and a virgin heroine.

Join my email list!

You can join my email list to be notified as soon as more books come out:
https://ruthannnordinauthorblog.com/sign-up-for-email-list/

All Books by Ruth Ann Nordin

(Chronological Order)
Regencies

<u>Marriage by Scandal Series</u>
The Earl's Inconvenient Wife
A Most Unsuitable Earl
His Reluctant Lady
The Earl's Scandalous Wife
<u>Marriage by Design Series</u>
Breaking the Rules
Nobody's Fool
A Deceptive Wager
<u>Standalone Regencies</u>
Her Counterfeit Husband (happens during A Most Unsuitable Earl)
An Earl In Time (A Fairytale Regency Romance)
<u>Marriage by Deceit Series</u>
The Earl's Secret Bargain
Love Lessons With the Duke
Ruined by the Earl
The Earl's Stolen Bride
<u>Marriage by Arrangement Series</u>
His Wicked Lady
Her Devilish Marquess

The Earl's Wallflower Bride
<u>Marriage by Bargain Series</u>
The Viscount's Runaway Bride
The Rake's Vow
Taming The Viscountess
If It Takes A Scandal
<u>Marriage by Fate Series</u>
The Reclusive Earl
Married In Haste
Make Believe Bride
The Perfect Duke
Kidnapping the Viscount
<u>Marriage by Fairytale Series</u>
The Marriage Contract
One Enchanted Evening
The Wedding Pact
Fairest of Them All
The Duke's Secluded Bride
<u>Marriage by Necessity Series</u>
A Perilous Marriage
The Cursed Earl
Heiress of Misfortune
<u>Marriage by Obligation Series</u>
Secret Admirer
Midnight Wedding
The Earl's Jilted Bride
Worth the Risk
Anyone But the Marquess

Historical Western Romances

<u>Pioneer Series</u>
Wagon Trail Bride
The Marriage Agreement

SECRET ADMIRER

Groom For Hire
Forced Into Marriage
<u>Nebraska Series</u>
Her Heart's Desire
A Bride for Tom
A Husband for Margaret
Eye of the Beholder
The Wrong Husband
Shotgun Groom
To Have and To Hold
Forever Yours
His Redeeming Bride
Isaac's Decision
<u>Misled Mail Order Brides Series</u>
The Bride Price
The Rejected Groom
The Perfect Wife
The Imperfect Husband
<u>Husbands for the Larson Sisters</u>
Nelly's Mail Order Husband
Perfectly Matched
Suitable for Marriage
Daisy's Prince Charming
<u>Wyoming Series</u>
The Outlaw's Bride
The Rancher's Bride
The Fugitive's Bride
The Loner's Bride
<u>Chance at Love Series</u>
The Convenient Mail Order Bride
The Mistaken Mail Order Bride
The Accidental Mail Order Bride

The Bargain Mail Order Bride
<u>Nebraska Prairie Series</u>
The Purchased Bride
The Bride's Choice
Interview for a Wife
<u>South Dakota Series</u>
Loving Eliza
Bid for a Bride
Bride of Second Chances
<u>Montana Collection</u>
Mitch's Win
Boaz's Wager
Patty's Gamble
Shane's Deal
<u>Native American Romance Series</u>
Restoring Hope
A Chance In Time
Brave Beginnings
Bound by Honor, Bound by Love
<u>Virginia Series</u>
An Unlikely Place for Love
The Cold Wife
An Inconvenient Marriage
Romancing Adrienne
<u>Standalone Historical Western Romances</u>
Falling In Love With Her Husband
Kent Ashton's Backstory
Catching Kent
His Convenient Wife
Meant To Be
The Mail Order Bride's Deception

Contemporary Romances

SECRET ADMIRER

<u>Omaha Series</u>
With This Ring, I Thee Dread
What Nathan Wants
Just Good Friends
<u>Across the Stars Series</u>
Suddenly a Bride
Runaway Bride
His Abducted Bride
<u>Standalone Contemporaries</u>
Substitute Bride

Thrillers

Return of the Aliens (Christian End-Times Novel)
Late One Night (flash fiction)
The Very True Legends of Ol' Man Wickleberry and his Demise - Ink Slingers' Anthology

Fantasies

<u>Enchanted Galaxy Series</u>
A Royal Engagement
Royal Hearts
The Royal Pursuit
Royal Heiress

Nonfiction

<u>Writing Tips Series</u>
11 Tips for New Writers
The Emotionally Engaging Character
Writing for Passion
Making a Realistic Publishing Schedule

Printed in the USA
CPSIA information can be obtained
at www.ICGtesting.com
LVHW010242260924
792206LV00026B/264